Virgin Gingelly

V. Sanjay Kumar owes this book to a baniya lineage that three generations before him have tried to obliterate by staying in Tamil Nadu. He has a tenuous hold on it, helped by language and a maternal side that stayed on in Uttar Pradesh. He grew up in Chennai in tenanted houses owned by Brahmins, absorbing their milieu and their predilections. Till date, he yearns for a childhood he never had in the Hindi heartland.

This is his second work of fiction. His first novel, *Artist, Undone* (Hachette India), was published in January 2012.

Praise for V. Sanjay Kumar

Virgin Gingelly

'Reading through *Virgin Gingelly* is much like taking a walk along with Sanjay, in the erstwhile Chennai of the author's memory.' – *Deccan Chronicle*

'This book is intelligently crafted and surely not about virgins or gingelly as the title deceptively suggests.' – *Asian Age*

*

Artist, Undone

'The author uses his own life and work as a springboard, vaulting into a seemingly messy situation and navigating it with humour, warmth and a certain special madness that only a creative soul can produce.' – *The Hindu*

‘A wickedly humorous book – finely written, marvellously layered, intricately crafted and psychologically curious. The book is about hell, of self-discovery, and the price of self-discovery.’ – *Deccan Herald*

‘Kumar breaks several conventional patterns of novel writing with *Artist, Undone*. One gets to see a lot of images in between and there is a mix of poetry, twisted prose and long dialogues. The narrative is not linear. Probably this is the first time someone has attempted this pattern in English fiction.’ – *Businessworld*

‘Sanjay Kumar’s *Artist, Undone* is a superb tale told with zest and cunning, a literary romp that both excites the reader and brings her or him to a sobering wisdom. Kumar wields the dagger of irreverence to telling effect, modulating a Salingeresque tonality... An elegant literary achievement!’ – Ranjit Hoskote, author of *Vanishing Acts: New and Selected Poems 1985-2005* and *I, Lalla: The Poems of Lal Ded*

Virgin Gingelly

V. Sanjay Kumar

hachette
INDIA

First published in 2014 by Hachette India
(Registered name: Hachette Book Publishing India Pvt. Ltd)
An Hachette UK company
www.hachetteindia.com

This edition published in 2016

SRD

P-ISBN: 978-93-5195-098-1
E-ISBN: 978-93-5195-034-9

Hachette Book Publishing India Pvt. Ltd
4th & 5th Floors, Corporate Centre,
Plot No. 94, Sector 44,
Gurgaon 122003, India

Typeset in Sabon 10.5/14.5
by Ram Das Lal, NCR Delhi

Printed and bound in India by Manipal Technologies Limited, Manipal

MIX
Paper from responsible sources
FSC™ C043100
FSC www.fsc.org

Call it an eye or an ear. She has it.
For Linika.

Contents

Badnaam Basti 1

Maatra 8

I The Chameleon

Wordless 14

Faasle 26

Parikrama 35

Langda 44

II The Vagabond

Rangaswamy I.I.T. Madras 54

Rangaswamy, Betrothal 67

III The Housewife

The Moneylender and the Priest 78

Asylum 87

Number 24 101

Half Ticket 113

Leaving Home 118

IV

The Function 130

V The Story

Kausalya Suprabhatham 138

VI The Runt
Ramanathan 156
Rainbow 162
Ashadu, Asingham 173
Valiban 183
White Lies 196

VII Murthy
Nullah 204
Uthama Puthiran 211

VIII
The Confession 228
My Dear Murthy 240

Acknowledgements 251

BADNAAM BASTI

ACCORDING TO RAGPICKERS' LORE I am the last of a curious breed, one that bears resemblance to the street where I live. They call me the scion of this small lane where trees are held up by wires and pavements have been walked on by roads. In the morning unshaven men clear their throats and shout my name. Coffee. It is the colour of my coat.

I was born in Delhi inside a municipal trash can that had tipped over and spilled. Some eight weeks before that I was conceived in its vicinity in public view. My father had a grimace I believe and my mother some fortitude and for a moment they were inseparable. One was facing the Qutub Minar and the other was eyeing Mehrauli. The ragpickers, who watched the union, rolled their eyes, threw some stones and left for the neighbouring street.

The manner of my making defines me more than my DNA. I come from a viscous concentrate, urgent and wakeful, served as a single helping. My parents were neither friends nor lovers. In fact, they had hardly met. This was a fleeting liaison; a fuck 'on the go' in this small hamlet in Delhi called Badnaam Basti. Delhi has these charming bastis that have survived the rapid sprawl of DDA complexes and private malls. This one is next to Mahipalpur.

It was past midnight. The debris had settled and in the momentary quiet took place this inarticulate conception.

There were three hoardings that stood in this basti for many months. The first of these, 'Hardik Swagat' welcomed you warmly. The second, 'Namastey IncredibleIndia' showed you a picture of the Taj Mahal, and the third, 'Humdo Hamaredo' asked you to use a condom whenever you felt animated. People came up to them, looked up and stared, and the men amongst them stood with feet apart and did their business.

It is no surprise that I look and behave like a street dog.

I am now in Chennai, a city that in many ways is a distance from Delhi. Our basti is a puram called Rainbow Colony. Its folk are aged, gentle and retired. They cannot see very well and they walk with difficulty. In the evening they discuss their medical histories and relate tales of their valour when confronted with needles and knives.

The street that divides Rainbow Colony is vile. It cannot be gentrified. It is an abode for sore thumbs like me from the North. I am in the midst of territory-marking to fend off battle-hungry street dogs. Out here they are called porkis. This street is a hard place. I know because it has given me swollen eyes and bleeding gums. I know because people stare. I don't have a name but I have a harelip.

I am not a chauvinist and I am not a pig but I like the sound of Badnaam Busty. It gives me the shivers. I can imagine her as a woman of repute, with jugs and resplendent rags and a rich history of sharing her bed. She would stay in a place like mine, a bad-ass locality that gives no quarter and could tear you in half. And we would rummage bins together for leftover bread and scour the stuff that baristas throw for that last drop of cappuccino.

* * *

At the intersection of a road junction and a sewer pipe is my home. There is a triangular space that has me. Somebody set up a shelter here for a road digging unit. There are three slanting poles that have been tied together with rope and a canvas sheet has been stretched over them. I moved in without fanfare. Inside, the pavement is my floor and a roadside grill is my sink.

I have very few belongings that I leave inside. There is me and my friend, a dog who comes and goes.

Four days ago a policeman came and peeped inside. Lucky for him I wasn't around. I would have got him by the leg. He went away. The next day the dog says, 'Dig a hole, quick.' I dug up a portion of the pavement and left a hole. 'That looks like work in progress,' says the dog with a wink. 'Now we are safe.' The dog curls up and sleeps on the hole as the earth is cooler inside it. The dog's name is Kumar. He is a gentleman. Unlike me he doesn't run after cars.

I arrived in this city from Delhi in the brake van of a train called the Deluxe Express. I was the king of Platform Number 8 in the Nizamuddin Railway Station and in one of life's strange haadsas I walked into the luggage van of a train and fell asleep. I was knocked about for more than a day.

When they opened the door at the Central Station, Chennai, I jumped out, blinked a few times and escaped. It was night and I ran the streets, fleeing from the locals and scrounging for food.

I miss Delhi. I miss the seasons, I miss the gehu roti titbits and I miss the Hindi sound of kutte kameenay.

Rainbow Colony is a middle-class preserve. It is a co-operative colony and most of its residents have wrinkled and greyed and look like murabbas. The houses are small and the compounds are miniscule. There is room outside to park a two-wheeler and a cycle and space for two people to stand and watch what happens on the road. In the morning the newspaper boy comes on a cycle and milk comes in a van. Walkers use the road, one end of which leads onto a prosperous crescent called Boat Club. That crescent has pedigreed dogs that are walked by watchmen. It is their toilet. In the morning all the bends on the road and the leftover sand piles from construction are littered by pedigreed brats. You can make out they are well fed.

The street where I live has blood. All the battles take place here. It is laughable. The territory is meek and the spoils are rotten but the dogs are hungry for love. There is nothing else to do and nobody plays with us. So a chase and a skirmish helps even if the prize is a mongrel. It gives meaning to life on that street. And it courses your blood.

The few young menfolk on the street are mean-spirited. They have stopped dreaming and their lives have yielded to pessimism. They shave poorly, read the *Indian Express*, spill the garbage and curse the sun. Their wives are tired of being careful. They have no vices other than watching soaps that are weird imitations of their wildest dreams. These women need make-up to hide their thoughts. Their lives maybe plain but their minds are hotbeds.

Good times come in small doses in Rainbow Colony and they are precious; as precious as jewellery, as silk sarees with gold brocade, as memorabilia of youth and stolen moments in front of a mirror. The outings happen once a week. Then the younger women bring out their finery, step onto the two-wheeler with flowers in their hair, clasp an arm around their men and look for recognition.

It is sad to see them return at night. They slink into their homes and lock their doors. Their windows have welded grills. The hopelessness of all this gets to me. I howl and it is night, so it sounds loud and clear. People don't like the sound. I get shouted at. All I mean to ask them is, 'What separates you? What separates you from me?'

I like the old folk on the road. They are the grandparents who sit and read the paper from cover to cover and argue over the middle. And then they hang about near the gate after the grandchildren have left for school and their parents to work. It is a quiet period and a time for reflection. The sun is out and it is getting warm. The road has trees on both sides and the shade is a boon. These men and women shout to each other across the street. They wear white cotton veshtis and white cotton jibbas. Footwear has happened all their life and now they are barefoot.

The front portions of their homes are well swept and the rubbish is neatly on the sides. I pick my way through that rubbish, and I have learnt. It is important to separate the plastic from the trash and eat the leftovers from those packets. I confess to leaving a mess behind. Kumar is a disdainful fellow. He merely scrounges. He picks only the bottles and the broken furniture, which he then trades for small change.

I dream of a Municipality truck. It is the one that looks like a giant cage. It is the one that sweeps the city clean of the dogs of war. When the Municipality truck appears Kumar turns his nose away from me. I run to the wigwam and hide. I hate trucks from the Municipality. I have seen some take friends away.

People have started giving me biscuits. They find joy in doing so. Some bring stale wholewheat and the more thoughtful bring fresh Marie. They like to stand and watch me eat. I try but cannot finish them all. Kumar is too proud. He will have none of them.

'Get down on all fours and yelp?' No. He will not be a beggar.

'I am not one either,' I inform him.

'Did I say that?'

'I am a performer. They like to see me eat.'

'Kumar!' shouts someone. Off goes Kumar. He is everybody's handy animal, not me. He fetches well, he cleans cars for small change and at a pinch he keeps guard. And he plays with the children. Nobody calls for me after the coffee is drunk. All the fights on the road have hurt my hide and scuffed my coat. I look beat-up. One ear is chewed and one leg hurts over stone.

'You are in a hard place,' Kumar tells me. 'You don't have a name (he means an ID), you don't have caste or creed (he means pedigree), you have no master (he means collar?) and you have no roots.'

'So what happens?'

He scratches his head and tries to look kind. 'You often get culled. You get taken away to the pound.'

He means well but it isn't a pleasant thought.

'Say something,' he says.

What is there to say?

'Don't fuck with my humanity,' I say.

* * *

I am writing all this down because my life has changed. Kumar the gentleman has found a job. His bearing has takers.

'One day I will come back for you,' he says as he leaves.

'I will be here,' I promise in return.

Before his dust has settled the diggers come. They have camped in my home. And they have dug up my hole. They are pulling thick cables. I am on my way to the Crescent to try my luck. Kumar told me that pedigreed dogs don't bite. But the watchmen throw stones. I will be outnumbered.

* * *

A week has passed. The Municipality truck has come again. I am slow and they get me. I take a last look before I leave. A Badnaam Basti. A dark place; it has given me swollen eyes and bleeding gums. You must have walked through it without knowing. You might have seen me there without noticing. It is a street with no name. But it has mood and it has gesture. And for the moment it has lost its son.

MAATRA

THE TROUBLE IS IN THE LEES, places where the weather cannot reach. I am seated erect under a pergola in a sheltered corner of this home in Cenotaph Road. My cane mooda has a backrest but the seat prickles my thighs. The evening sun has petered out near the pathway. Not a leaf stirs. The atmosphere scarches for an accomplice. It finds me, quiet, reflective and with a dwindling stash of words. It is a time to lift some heft and read *War and Peace*.

My hand journeys to a drink made from grain and my friend for the evening looks on balefully as I snaffle the first. He has come from a Gents' Beauty Parlour, glistening, with a clean shave of the head.

'Raat baaki hai,' says Guptaji as I pour my second.

Slow down, he implies. I try.

'You should go for a teerth yatra,' says Guptaji, for the nth time. 'Pilgrimages can be cleansing, trust me.'

'I don't need such journeys,' I reply.

Just this morning I had looked in alarm at a milestone that had been transformed into a lingam. Manjal and kumkum had erased the distance to Dindigul. A family had parked their scooter and was conducting an aarti in front of the stone. The woman looked hopeful, placing some flowers at this roadside deity, her eyes closed and her faith touching. I had returned disturbed, having seen the man, her husband, and knowing that no good would come from entreaty.

'How long can I keep coming here just to keep you company?' asks Guptaji.

Kind of him to come but why should I say it? He is a singleton in any case, a mysterious jack who holds his playing cards close but easily dispenses with their portents. He is also a reckless bastard who chews tobacco throughout the day, building an oral history that will one day script his death.

A police car drives past us blowing a siren. Round the bend it goes. Must be Inspector Murthy hurrying for no reason and alerting the low-life. Red light flashes from his jeep and reflects on my house windows.

'He does that every other day just to let me know. He doesn't trust me.'

'Shri Murthy?'

I nod and I smile examining my hands. 'He says he hasn't understood me. He doesn't approve of what happens around me.'

Guptaji is quizzical but doesn't prod.

'He also says my eyes are evil and my thoughts are halaal.'

'There are enough career thieves in the vicinity,' says Guptaji. 'But you are the one who went to jail. At least now you are free.'

Free? Talk to me about the confines of an interior space.

We sit around aimlessly. If there was a moon we would have probably watched it rise.

'Kumar babu, you should get married again,' he says, after my third drink. 'It is not healthy. All you do is sit and write.'

Enough time has elapsed. Words have flown. As a writer I forage for loot in Rainbow Colony, a short walk away. The unlatched window, the unlocked balcony, the careless verandah screen or the showy glass door, each yield to my curiosity. Tree branches overhang the boundary walls of these houses and provide a leg-up to balconies.

Guptaji pulls out the first of his aseptic packets. He peels one and empties the contents into his mouth, tapping till the last puff of dust descends. One part betel, one part zarda and one part catechu; chew it, spit it. Live the high, die the death. I drink some more till the liquor hits. He chews steadily. After another hour we take risks. I go first.

'Let me start with a confession. Eight years have passed since I killed someone.'

* * *

I am drunk. My voice is down to a whisper.

'Some things did take place. They are recorded as facts; handwritten in Police Records in the Kotturpuram Police Station in a register that I have seen. I have countersigned the pages under duress. From there it will go to the courthouse in Parry's Corner and then to the tea house of the August moon.'

Guptaji takes a paan break. The paan is a saada with star, salli supari and keemam. I take one too. It is delicious. Harsh on the throat, spite on the tongue and a bitter finish at the very end.

'Jai Shri Ram,' mumbles Guptaji, looking replete. He has the makings of a mountain sadhu. 'What were you saying?'

I slur. I speak as if I am reading what I have written.

'My writing comes to me like bits and pieces in a puzzle. I was young once and even then I couldn't piece it together. If people have patience, like I do, then they will know that an easy narrative is not to be trusted.'

I write people in my own image. Sincerely yours. Very truly. It is the oldest trick in the book. I write about the city like it is mine. Chennai is not my natural home but it is the glue that holds me together. The street that took hold of me is a small one but it kept me sane. It has a house where I live. No. 24. It is the only place I will stake a claim for. The house had a wife whose disappearance belied her nature. She was a woman of substance.

'I should write this book in Hindi,' I mumble. 'Or Tamil.'

'Raat baaki hai, Kumar babu,' says Guptaji. 'Write a classic.'

Hail the Dravidian night. Follow the Southern Cross. There is virtue left to be won. But the Convents are dying and the Queen's English rots on Casa Major Road. The locals are making their electric dreams into minsara kanavu. The nights belong to old watchmen like Periaswamy who sit amongst clouds of mosquito repellents. Periaswamy, wide-eyed as an owl, goes past our gate. He raps the doors and windows and the road for good measure. He is a clever man. He knows that sleep and the death of duty come from natural causes.

'Tell me about yourself,' says Guptaji. 'What was Kumar like when he was young?'

I

THE CHAMELEON

WORDLESS

MRS ABHYANKAR SAYS THIS IS HER WORST POSTING. This one was born out of the inertia of a conditioned life. Her husband Colonel Abhyankar was posted as Commanding Officer in the Signals Regiment in places like Jabalpur, Mhow, Palam, Shimla and finally Chennai. They lived well. The houses were in secure enclaves, the grounds were lavish, the help was plentiful and the Officer's Mess took care of their social requirements. Chennai was a quiet posting.

It was just another sunny day in Chennai when the Colonel died.

Overnight, the tight circle of the Army escarpment was broken; the elastic went limp and Mrs Abhyankar's life sagged in the middle. Her husband had purchased a flat in Chennai on a whim, perhaps to keep the money aside, locked into real estate as a hedge against inflation. When he passed away, she moved into this civilian locality that was in the heart of the city. It was far removed from the Enclave. This was murky water. This was an insecure world full of grasping piranhas and finless great whites. This India was a nation of shopkeepers.

Ironically, at a time when she was free of encumbrance and could do what she liked, she felt hemmed in.

Three years she stayed alone, speaking in undertones to the departed life.

'I am a goldfish that is searching for a bowl in this ocean,' she said.

She had three bedrooms, a living/dining and a balcony where she spent her time contemplating this living Hell. She was forty-eight years old when I arrived at her door in response to an ad that said 'Room to let'. When she opened the door that evening our eyes met.

'What do you do?' she asked, standing at the door.

'I write,' I said. I must have looked like a stray because she hesitated. 'My unpublished book is called *Dogs are People Like You and Me*.'

'I see. And what is the first chapter?'

'Badnaam Basti,' I replied.

She asked me no more questions. She took me to the guest room and said, 'Dinner begins at 7 p.m. Don't be late.'

I remembered later what she wore: a white gown held at the waist and a pale pink slip through which her nipples showed.

* * *

I am twenty-eight years old. I wish to write. So far I have progressed thrice to page 50. Page 50 is a crossroad where strangers beckon and plot lines collide. I arrive and in the absence of further discourse I return. Someone told me that I needed to live a life before I could write things like stories and longreads called novels. Someone asked me to take up journalism. These suggestions are in a box along with my unfinished work.

Mrs Abhyankar, I discovered, has been hard-coded in the ways of defence households. Afternoons, she gets up from her charpoy and proceeds to the teapoy. The lady, and she is one, still practises ceremony. Tea is served in a pot by the cook, sandwiches have their edges trimmed, hair is dyed scrupulously by a maid, clothes are pressed and stowed in order and her shoes have leather that is too proud to be creased. In the night she asks absently for Ram Singh and Tej Bahadur, orderlies who served her well. Good men she left behind in the departed life.

'Could you change this light bulb?'

Yesterday it was, Could you hammer this nail?

I hitch up my shorts, stand on the small ladder and stretch. She comes up close, ostensibly, to hold the ladder. This is frivolous; the third time in a week that I have climbed a stair while she has hovered at the stepwell of her imagination.

She likes me around her in the evening hours. Whatever else I do I have to be with her most days for drinks and dinner. Some days other things happen as well; or so say the neighbours. Tamilian tongues wag in the building stairwells and hands are wrung near the clothes lines. It doesn't help that I can be found mornings, lounging in the corridors or leaning on the wall in my tight sleeveless T's and bulging boxers. I have tousled hair and a slow wink that keeps pulses in good spirit in the neighbourhood.

My landlady is a former English Literature teacher. She

is well read and still puts away a book a day. Yet she yearns for words of love. There is something forlorn about her that makes me stay in this place. I want to shake her out of what she is in. What she is living is a fucking ode to the departed life.

'What kind of day is it outside?' she asks.

Let me see. Oscar Wilde is writing epitaphs and Coldplay is singing anthems.

'An ordinary day,' I reply.

'Draw the blinds, will you, please.'

She has a running battle with age. Age is her sworn enemy and she keeps it at bay. Yoga, light workouts, Oil of Olay, wheatgrass, tasteless juices, and all the recommended diets find their way into her day. She is well preserved. I wish she was better turned out. She wears frippery and lace that were handmade when that form had a following.

Every inch of her house is a setting from the previous generation. It is an apartment in a four-storey structure. The rear of the building faces a small park, which is a haven for birds and urban sanity. Her house is an extension of her being; well maintained but a little dated. I stand out in all this as her one aberration.

I am beginning to notice where I stand.

'You are so grounded,' she says.

I am.

'You should challenge your reality. All writers do.'

I should.

'Life could be surreal if you tried.'

Surreal?

'Time would melt like Dali; Duchamp would descend from your staircase to your loo.'

She laughs as she spots my open mouth.

'Why are you so stingy with words?'

Am I?

I have a need to be exact. I chisel language. I have to prise it out of my teeth. Each word has to count, each barb has to sting.

'In the words of the Bard...' I begin.

And I forget.

I forget what people have said. I am poor with verbatim.

* * *

I walked away from her to the room she has given me. It used to be the guest room and it serves as my accommodation. This paying guest now comes free. She stopped taking money from me a couple of years ago. Despite occasional misgivings I have stayed on.

Today I hit page 30, ground to a halt, floundered with some openings and then trudged back. I tried to redo an earlier effort that had failed and could not save it. It felt like there was a hole in my head. Only a domestic frenzy would take my mind out of this hole. I sorted clothes for a couple of hours. I ironed them till the hissing steam burnt my face. I swept and swabbed. I ran out of routine.

This is not the first time I have blanked out.

When I returned to the living room in the evening, she was wearing a nightdress that swayed open dangerously. She held a drink in her left hand. A bottle of rum and a bottle of soda lay on the table. Some evenings she couldn't wait to get started.

'What kept you?' she slurred.

I struggled with my phrasing.

She sighed. 'Help yourself.'

I did. She watched me pour and dared me to look down the front of her dress to her drooping breasts and her flat stomach. I watched the bubbles rise and raised a toast to her navel.

'As you grow older, you speak less,' she said. 'It is scientifically proven. Every year we eat some of our words. We chew them and very few survive.'

'Should I play some music?' She nodded. Her music belonged to ten years ago, a time when her only son was still alive. It stopped the year they moved to Chennai when he went for an army operation at a border post and was killed. She has kept his room as it was. Every night she fluffed the pillows and hoped they would lose shape.

'What hope is there for the language of loss?' she asked.

I was hard-pressed to say something.

'You will go from bad to worse. In another five years you will learn to grunt.'

She is never done with her drinking. I poured her another. I could smell the cologne behind her ears. She held my hand and I shook myself free.

'Words come to me sometimes, in a train of thought...' I said.

'Bugger that,' she said. 'Bugger your train.'

I should have left. If I spoke from exasperation, language would repent.

'What do you want from me?' I asked her.

'I want you to try.'

She folded my fingers.

'Carry on.'

She placed my hand on her shoulder. We moved closer.

'Now talk.'

I couldn't. She was getting under my skin.

'I could write before I met you,' I shouted.

I thought I shouted. Her face crumbled.

* * *

My room overlooks the park. A tree nudges at my window and leaves fall in when the sea breeze sets in. I have a single bed and two pillows. Propped on them, I see time through a window. It is early afternoon. The rest of the day looms and I have to get away.

I go shopping for words. I am a bookshop addict. I need to roam among shelves and scan the titles. I meet uncertainty at the poetry section. Amongst literature there is disdain. Even humble prose looks askance at my browsing. Fellow browsers show their age. They read as they stand. They find passages from a time well spent.

My book buying reveals my problem. I go for books that are not conventional. I go for the lesser known, the slightly exotic and the differently phrased.

The first page should have metaphor, unusual language and one thing bold.

'You always seem to slink in,' says the bookstore owner. He has appeared suddenly by my side.

Slink in?

'You hold a book as if you are hiding it.'

Hiding?

'Have you read *Eats, Shoots and Leaves*?

I shake my head. I wait for him to go away. He doesn't oblige.

'Are you looking for something specific?' he asks finally.

'I am looking for a book called *How to Lose Your Muse*. Do you have it?'

How could he? I was still writing it.

I get forced into buying a book. I carry it with me reluctantly in a plastic bag. It adds weight as I walk and it feels heavy by the time I reach home. I place it in my bookcase between Italo Calvino and Marcus Zusak. There it will gather dust.

'You have bought another book?' asks the household.

I can hear the shelves groaning, I can hear the unread authors groaning.

I read aloud from the book I bought. It is by Jeanette Winterson.

'Book collecting is an obsession, an occupation, a disease, an addiction, a fascination, an absurdity, a fate. It is not a hobby. Those who do it must do it. Those who do not do it, think of it as a cousin of stamp collecting, a sister of the trophy cabinet, bastard of a sound bank account and a weak mind.'

* * *

'Literature is for the seriously indulgent.'

Titter from the front row. Well, only the front row is occupied and those are the acolytes. They are bespectacled, frizzy-haired women with a stance.

'Who reads literature?'

The acolytes at book readings have the power these days. They raise their hands in mock support. My hand hides in my pocket.

'I meant, in general. Who in this befuddled world reads

literature? I know people with shelves who buy it and I know of swallows who skim it.'

One acolyte has a shapely arm. It comes into view. The silk sleeve slides down a waxed hand revealing a silver ring, painted nails and a gold bracelet.

'Yes, my dear.'

I switch off at this familiarity. Why am I here? I am in the last of five benches. I am in the chair near the door. I have not made eye contact with the author but I am embarrassed about slinking away.

'Do you have something to add?' I hear. They are looking at me. I asked for it.

'Sir,' I say. 'Can you write literature for the masses?'

The acolytes want to spring to his defence but he holds up a hand. I can see his palm and his lifeline.

'Why do you ask?' he says. He really wants to know.

'Nobody in my colony has read *Hamlet*,' I reply.

He is nonplussed.

'It is a long play,' he blurts finally. And then a bulb glows in his head. 'What about Kalidas?' he asks.

I shake my head.

'Literature has always been accessible,' he mumbles. He flips pages of his own book. 'I must examine my language.'

I walk up to him for a private moment.

'Have you ever lost your muse?' I ask him.

* * *

What have I brought for her?

Travail.

I stand behind her. She likes facing a mirror. It is an oval mirror with a retro frame painted white. The wall behind me is a deep burgundy. Her face is framed like a portrait of yore. That is how she likes it; she and time are frozen compatriots.

I cannot understand why I am lost for words. She does this to me. I am a writer. There is proof that you are reading.

She asks me to move away. She picks a scarf that complements her skin tone and her mood. She dons it. And she adds three black dots to her forehead.

'Follow me.'

That's what I do.

She leads me to her bookshelf and she flips through a few books till she finds it. *Lady Chatterley's Lover.*

Beautiful and tender and as frail as the naked self, she murmurs.

She caresses the cover. I can hear birdsong in the background and a caw from a crow.

She is harsh.

'Kumar, your life is a mere adaptation. You walked out from the pages of a book that you read. Look at you. You are just a bloody actor.'

It was a time to say it. It was what I did to her in bed.

'Copy that,' I mumble instead.

* * *

Before you cave in, throw some rocks.

She wants music and I have picked the shehnai, which is a difficult listen, hoping to get away.

'When will the music start?' she asks.

I am hearing Bismillah Khan speak. For a musician, he has a reedy voice. His accent saves him; it comes from the root of a neem tree. That tree gives shade in Benares. She wants to walk away and almost does but the old man has presence.

He wears his cap and lifts the instrument to his lips. It belongs to him more than his hands.

Khan Saheb closes his eyes and pouts. The first note from the shehnai is pure; it pierces the air you breathe. This is sound from the centuries, sound that is rooted and compelling.

Malkauns.

Man changes into Messiah.

'Magical and truly beguiling,' says my muse.

This is not going as per plan. She is starry-eyed.

'We should get married,' she says.

Damn.

Khan Saheb, will this pass?

* * *

A time to purge, a time to leach; it was time to face the world outside. I had a backpack of notebooks and a few revisions in my head. At a nearby coffee outlet I sat on a sofa and smelt cappuccino. The first sentence took shape on the napkin.

If you treat the past as Karma, there are no debts to pay.

I looked at myself in the mirrored wall of the coffee shop. Nothing had changed outwardly, there was no epiphany between my ears and it was clear as daylight that I wasn't the infant they called Destiny's Child.

Time to head back one last time. I ran up the stairs two at a time and arrived breathless and rang the bell. She was expressionless as I brushed past her and walked into her son's room. She followed me. His room was as he had left it, it seemed. I needed to see what the young fellow had left behind before he left for that mission. I was looking for the maps of a young mind.

He had left behind a drawer full of things to be rummaged. Socks, route maps, pencils, shavings, a badge, some rope, remedies for cold, some second thoughts and a notepad full of misgivings. I flipped through the notepad and his mother flinched. Even as she watched and before she could react I crawled into her son's bed and rested my head. The pillow lost its shape.

'Mrs Abhyankar,' I said before I left. She didn't react. 'I am not old enough to be your husband nor young enough to be your son.'

Her face still lacked expression. I tried again.

'Life is your pillow, Mrs Abhyankar. It takes from you and loses shape.'

FAASLE

IT WAS A MAGNIFICENT SUNRISE. The sun broke through a bank of clouds on the horizon. The light caught up with grief. There were bodies on the beach, washed ashore, awaiting disposal. People waited for those who hadn't returned. Nearby lay the overturned boat looking like a beached whale, its rafters splintered like a busted ribcage. Two men were still at sea, missing. They were the younger ones.

'The stronger swimmers come in last,' said Rangaswamy. He was smoking a loosely filled cigarette, looking calm and unaffected.

'That sounds fucking kevalam,' I replied.

'Let us get away,' said my tactless friend.

I looked back as we walked away. The anxious fishing village, the meen kuppam waited by the shoreline, breast-beating, wailing and cursing. I had heard it before on the streets of Madras. The words were the same; thevadiya the Tamil whore and koodi the Tamil cunt, dredged up from the gutter where the urban found expression. The Gods bore the brunt of the swearing. God was a paavam in this land that saw the hungry tide, the tsunami.

But this was different.

I knew that every year the sands of the Marina and the Elliots beach were cleaned. And every year fun and frolic lead to someone swimming and getting pulled away, never to return.

Somehow this was different.

'It seems unfair,' I said to those willing to listen. 'That those who make a living from the sea should be consumed by it.'

* * *

My city slept at 9 and took birth at 5. It was a visible city. In its nooks and by-lanes, in its wide open artery called Mount Road, on the sacred Mount of Saint Thomas, amongst the Thousand Lights of a Mosque, in the weedy temple tank near Kapaleeswar, in the hearts and minds of a Dravidian cult and a Brahmin pocket, the city lived. It took shape slowly. The gentry were plodders accustomed to a life that had few demands, in a drowsy climate that took few prisoners. It had character. The mould was ancient and the pigment was tan. Visitors marvelled at its studied pace. People have time here, they exclaimed.

'In this city,' says Rangaswamy, 'if you do not hurry to get anywhere you get there sooner.'

He looks spaced out.

Madras has always had an enormous beach and its sands stretch beyond the shore into people's homes, blown by the afternoon breeze and favoured by the citizens as a compound surface on which they grow sturdy plants like crotons and the riotous bougainvillea. The compound permitting, there is a neem tree for health, a tamarind tree for taste and a smaller lemon tree for seasoning.

Rangaswamy blows the shankh in the manner of a priest. This large conch shell has a piercing sound. As a child I fitted it into my palm and held it close to my ear. I could hear the waves of the Bay that it came from. The thought amazed me. Ranga has no nicety. He raises the conch shell to his lips, adapts a forlorn air and imitates the rise and fall note of the death march to the ghat. The sound is a sign of mortality and the neighbours scream at him for this grim reminder.

To live in this city is to die in this city. Reading the obituary column in *The Hindu* is a pastime. It shows old men and women in black and white pictures; some look grim and a few grin.

'Rangan attained Acharyan Thiruvadi,' says Ranga, pinpointing Rangan on the page.

'Shantha is remembered with tears.'

'Pattammal attained sivalokaprapti.'

'Ramamurthi merely expired.'

All were deeply mourned. And then we saw one of a young girl whose DOD exceeded DOB by a few. She smiles at us.

'Why on earth?' says Ranga. He is fucking moved. He puts away the shankh.

I came to this city by accident. An uncle fell ill in Madras, so my father was asked if he could move in and replace him in the business. My parents took the Rameswaram Express train to Chennai with three suitcases and three sleeper bags. They opened them in a crowded first floor in Royapettah, a commercial place that abutted shops and made no pretence about being tony.

According to my uncle, who reads things like leaves, it was pre-ordained. My jaadagam says I will live and die here. What the fuck, Guptaji? How can these ornery planets pass this sentence for a speck like me?

'Piss on your jaadagam,' suggests Ranga. He is serious.

'Guptaji,' he mocks. 'A horoscope is a suvidha; like a shauchalaya.'

* * *

I write. My school for writing has no walls and no chamber. It has a ghost. His name is Rangaswamy. He stands beside me and watches. I can feel his gaze and I can hear his reproach. Rangaswamy is the man I will never be and so he defines me. This chap is a risqué fellow with a glad eye; a hedonist, he lives a life that belies mine.

'You are not unique,' he tells me.

'You are the only one who matters,' he tells me again and again. 'Can't you see? The rest of humanity are self-serving bastards.'

'You want some grass?' he asks, as an afterthought.

I knew a musician who lost it mid-career. He was my good friend in his worst years when he couldn't piece it together like he used to. He would come home and moon about. I asked him why. I kept asking him. Finally he blurted, 'Ever since I have begun to listen, I have lost it.'

'I know exactly what you mean,' says Ranga. They used to be smoking buddies. Ranga looks at me now like I am a younger sibling and he is in some way responsible for me.

'One day you will lose it too,' he says. 'I promise.'

* * *

As a student of history I was a failure. We were in a one-year Pre-University programme, a prelude to greater things. Ranga was trying out for IIT and I was biding my time. In a class of 30, 28 studied monuments; I studied ruin. Ranga did not study at all. He travelled instead. He travelled to places we read about and told us we knew nothing.

'The "ravages of time" sounds grand to me,' I wrote in my college essay. 'This version of reality is not bleak, it is enervating.'

'Have you also been smoking?' asked my teacher.

On our visits to Delhi in the summers I would be transfixed by the Purana Qila, the fort that crumbled, and not by the freshly painted, fully scrubbed and rampart-repaired Red Fort. Purana Qila cannot be glossed over. This was terroir, a contoured landscape that resisted like its inhabitants did. This was history.

'The true monuments of history are those that we call ruins,' I wrote. 'Like Purana Qila.'

'Not the Red Fort?' asked my teacher.

'The Red Fort is a lovingly restored disaster, a botoxed baby,' I wrote.

My grade was dropping by the sentence. Ranga loved it.

Call it a failing but I liked staying with old people, people who aged badly, who let life leave its mark. I could spend hours reading their faces.

'History should not hide or be covered,' I concluded. 'History should be proud and show its age.'

* * *

When Ranga smokes, he dreams. He says that one day I will kill someone. He will not tell me whom.

'You need to live your life, Kumar,' he shouts. 'The stuff of your dreams won't do it.'

'Write,' he shouts, standing over me. My mother comes into the room that very moment and opens the windows. Smoke billows out as she stands and stares at Ranga.

'Maami,' he begins. 'Mannikkanum.'

He gets down on his knees, clearly contrite and cleans the dropped ash. He makes a show of emptying his pockets, pops a menthol into his mouth and in a moment that takes her by surprise, hugs her tight.

'Maami,' he says again. He doesn't let go of her. I feel a pang of something I cannot define.

* * *

I look like a child, younger than my years. But I was born old. My feelings are staid and my urges are quelled by a Catholic School that made morals a science. I seek approval from a man who could cast shadows at will. He stands with his back to me, torn, it seems, between his sullen nature and his family. He is my father. In my growing years he was a spent force who took away the sun.

My father has a masthead on which he writes. He wrote just one word in my presence. He did not have to say it, the look was enough. Kevalam. Kevalam means merely. It is a condescending view. 'You are beneath me,' says Kevalam. Colloquially, I was a piece of shit.

'It is natural for a father to hate his son,' says Ranga. He sounds like he knows everything.

The one bold move my father made was to marry a Tamilian girl. And then he withdrew, dug a moat around himself and pulled up the drawbridge. The business went to seed. His was a life that begged for a reason. My mother bore me and I saved her. We had each other in this house of contempt where nothing was good enough. To understand my mother I had to look at her forebears, a line-up of women of unfulfilled potential. They made a line from the kitchen to the rear where a granite washing stone and a hand pump had survived.

I know of no women who inscribe their mastheads. They draw, they paint and this is how they describe the world they inhabit. My mother painted a forest in which she hid. She is called Kamala, the lotus on which the Goddess of Wealth resides.

'Your mother is not a Kamala,' says Ranga. 'She is a Kasturi.'

Kasturi is the fragrance of musk.

'It resides within her,' says my friend.

I reside between these two worlds, Kasturi and Kevalam; one is a fragrance and the other a contemptuous view. I spent my childhood in the kitchen on the cusp, led by the nose and looked down upon.

Writing about old men is what I do. My old men mix wisdom with spite. These ornery codgers and curmudgeons hang about in my by-lanes in Rainbow Colony.

'Desperate buggers,' says Ranga. 'Look at them. They look like dead coral.'

Many of them have Ambassador cars with quirky gears that engage moodily. They walk tenderly, favouring one leg and then another, holding on to ledges, lamp-posts and dustbins. Their conversation is often about aches and pains.

'Skunks,' sums up Ranga, barely suppressing his mirth.

'They move like skunks.' His left arm jerks right. Higgledy. And his right arm jerks left. Piggledy. 'They smell like skunks as well,' he shouts as one old man farts.

The men scowl at us as we sit and watch them and hear them complain. Rainbow Colony is filled with these wrinkled bad-asses. Their morning constitutional is forced. They walk in circles in D'Monte Park. It is a small circle.

'Watch them unhinge,' whispers Ranga.

'L4,' says one holding his side. He looks crooked.

'L5,' says another bending over and trying to straighten.

After sixty, living is back breaking.

'The joyous invertebrates will take over this earth,' I declare.

My father walks by unexpectedly. I catch my breath. All that I was, was conveyed with one look.

'Why do you take it?' whispers Ranga.

I was culpable. I was proof that this family was pudding.

'I am no longer worried of all that I am,' I tell him. 'All that I will be takes the cake.'

* * *

This beach has been with Madras through the centuries. Every day the tide tries to claim it. It comes in waves and foams at the lip and the sands merely shift and somehow the large sandy enclave remains. But something has changed at the Marina. I find people, my people, walking and running and on weekends visiting for a sundal and an ice cream and for the sheer pleasure of dipping feet into water that has a sense of play. The change is within me as well. There is no time for lying on the sand, sunny side up. It seems the age for paranoia has been lowered. In the constricts of a colony and in the confines of homes people still deliver day upon day of life. It is all in the living.

We stand amidst shrubbery in Nageswara Rao Park in Mylapore. A refuse truck draws alongside and emits a Municipal belch. A few skins and packets break free from the rear. Ranga smokes and delivers one for the road.

'This used to be a garden we were in,' he breathes. 'Now it is compost.'

PARIKRAMA

You live hard, play hard. Life is a bitch, you say and join the club. You need a drink, a double shot and a vacation you never got.

Perched on your ladder, look me down; I am where I was, unfolding, unravelling.

I live my life in alaap time. I ride contours, I breathe nuance. I make out in this complete lack of substance.

I am a sucker for anything that holds me in the tip of thumb and forefinger. Like dope.

I wrote this in the city that taught me fuck. This is where I spent my interregnum; a city that has been carelessly brought up. I should have lived it in its teens, taken from its sepia moments that lie pressed between sheets. All I got was a middle-aged dowager; a frayed city, soaped, rinsed and wrung out to dry with wrinkles that won't go away. Mumbai is an ode to itself. What's left is khichdi bhasha, bhel-puri aesthetic and a grasping immigrant culture.

I found something in that city. I had to sift through the commonplace and live that miracle they called daily life. I was worked upon. The city is every inch a clichéd Maya Nagri; everybody dreams and some get rich. Nobody here likes to lose. Ten years in its backwaters and I was a goner. The upbringing of Chennai was gone, the baniya heartland sensibility of my forebears was gone and pretty much most of my hair was gone. I honed a few weapons: attitude, confidence and mostly the kind of irreverence that people would find precocious and irritating.

My name is Kumar. It is such a commonplace name.

I returned to Chennai vastly superior. The local populace was in a time warp. It was obvious, looking at them, that fashion here was not fashionable, culture was mostly leftovers and the pace of life was Mumbai-retiree. There was just one rock star in Chennai and that was me; and guess what, I couldn't sing. The city would have to adjust, my neighbours would have to take it and my friends of the past years would have to adapt.

One part of me still speaks Tamil. It lurks in me like a strange misdemeanour. There is a portion in my recipe that no ladle will reach. It is the dried crust of years of schooling in a Tamil-medium school in Madurai. That small pallikudam with a banyan tree had encircled some brain matter that refused to mingle. When it reared its head it was fearsome. The fusillade of Tamil that I was capable of could surprise reverends like Thiruvalluvar and Kannagi. I had given vent to it in the narrow lanes of Thiruvellikeni, on the platforms of Egmore Railway Station and on the sands of the Marina. Every time my intemperate wit had me in trouble I had this to fall back upon. I could speak like a native of an era that preceded the locals. My Tamizh belonged to the men and women who had shielded this land from the desis, the Hindi pasangas, the imposing types from the North; the illiterate fuckers who had no idea of Dravidian history that preceded their own.

People invoke feeling in others. It is a chemistry thing. They cannot help it. I would like to invoke laughter and admiration but the dice in my tumbler settled on hate. Hate is a curious thing; it is bad for a cocktail. I had this hate thing following me wherever I went; strong feelings, sometimes because of what I said or did, other times for no reason. People wanted to tear my guts out. I could see it in their eyes. I could see what bile can do to people of small means.

Let me say this slowly: Hate is skin deep.

Skin has colour. Karuppu means black. Vellai means white. In between is smoke and Lacto Calamine. The sun has no screen in the South and is the root cause of this pohai-smoked tinge to the local noir. Inside the rathham is the same, man. The local dudes know it, for when aruvaals split skin, inside was the same in any language; bloody bled.

Language has colour. There is no shying away from it. Language has a colour code that comes from the way it sounds to the ear, the way it woos, the way it makes love, the manner of its curse and the way it greets death. Some colours are from the earth, some from the sky, some from the wind and some from the rain. Tamizh comes from the sun; pure unadulterated sun. It has a burnish and it has a tan and it has baked in layers. The zha sound defines this language in my ear. Not da and not ra and not ha but a rich pastry from it all, made like a bebinca or a dol-dol or further south like a Mangalore halwa. It is the concentrate of ingredient and richness of colour that makes Tamil a noir language.

Some part of me likes noir. It is a separate life form. Who do I explain this to?

* * *

I ran over a leg today. I was driving a small car that has a large A pillar. There is a black vertical wedge next to my shoulder that intrudes into my line of sight. So if someone approaches from the right at a T-junction when you are wishing to turn right as well, you are momentarily blinded. A two-wheeler bearing a man called Balan and his girl called Rani was shielded by my A pillar. They were taking a wide turn because Balan was impressing Rani. Rani was holding onto his left hip and right shoulder. Balan's left knee was close to the ground. The funny thing is I didn't feel a thing. The bike skidded, Balan's right leg shot out, I swerved and my front right wheel ran over his leg. My car is a light metal Japanese mini and our combined weight couldn't do more than bruise his leg badly. He was fit enough to hop up, gather his pride, give in to his rage, come up to my window, yank me by the collar and blow into my face.

He hit me in a funny way. It wasn't a punch; it was more like a slap. My spectacles dug into my nose and came off, my hair was ruffled and my cheek bore the brunt. Rani was behind him and our eyes met. She looked ruffled. I got out of my car and saw the sprawled bike. Balan was as tall as a tree. I looked up at him and decided I would not touch him. There were two autorickshaw drivers and a few cyclists that had gathered and Man in Car was always wrong and poor Guy on Bike with Girl was always the victim.

Balan slapped me again. He had to bend down to do so and I could see him wince. His leg must have hurt. The crowd was on his side and that gave him courage. It took a lot out of me to keep my hands by my side.

I heard myself speak. 'Saale, harami ke aulad,' I began.

I saw his eyes widen.

'Teri jaan khatre me hai, gaandu,' I added.

This cannot be happening, I thought. The rowdies gathered, heard me speak Hindi, and started to push me around. I felt as if I was in another world and as they encircled me I kept speaking. After every blow I let them know in chaste Hindi that their mothers and sisters were my victims. I pointed just to confirm: 'Teri maa aur teri behen.'

The sound of a police whistle sounded absurd, the sound of my head hitting the ground sounded loud. Even as I fell I let my right leg come up with force and catch Balan below the belt. Things were woozy thereafter.

* * *

I am held. I am turned around. The edges are tested. I am held up against the light. They let go. The free fall wakes me up. I will never know if I shattered. But there is glass all over Mount Road near the flyover. I have hit someone again.

'Kumar?'

The speakerphone crackles and breaks my dream.

'Choothya from Matunga? You think you are special?'

My hand searches for something, anything. A green light is blinking. At the count of three the call cuts off abruptly, followed by a ringtone. The green light dies. Sweat drips off my forehead into the dark. The bloody weather in Chennai; this is not the place of my birth.

He will call again. They always do; these anonymous callers. I reach under my pillow and find my watch.

5 a.m. It is a muggy morning because the rain threatened but never fell. I have slept alone in a room that is my den. I listen to my breath. Somewhere an early bird is singing a Suprabhatham, a Venkatesa Suprabhatham.

'Kaushalya supraja rama...' it begins. For once I am not lulled.

5.30 a.m. and I am still awake. I can hear Seergazhi Govindrajan; his rustic entreaty evokes a seasonal image of bearded men in black veshtis walking up a hill. It must be the time for the Sabarimalai pilgrimage.

The second call is shrill.

'Kumar? Dai English type. Bloody torn-jeans fellow.'

A longer wait, this time to let me know. Sleep drifts by.

The eagle in the sky circles and the circle funnels and descends. The sound of my breath, the sound of descent: sounds of eavesdropping. I can hear electronic whispers.

I move my right hand to break the thought that someone alive is ruling my moment. I engage the answering service and bury my head under the pillow.

6 a.m. The speakerphone engages.

'If you would like to leave your name and number...'

He doesn't call my name.

I pad up to the machine and breathe.

Come on behenchod; circle the string. Cast the line now.

'Kumar? Dai Hindi porrikki.'

I hover in darkness.

'We have your address da. We will come and get you.'

Someone knocks on my door. The timing is startling. I walk carefully and the peephole shows nothing. I open the door and no one stands outside but at my feet I find a street dog that bears my collar. It lies down. I fall to my knees.

* * *

I visit the temples of Chennai once every year. I have many relatives here and they have eyes and ears. But I come in the guise of a Bombay lad, dressed like a Breach Candy dude. I look spoilt at the edges and I stand out like an outsider. Today I am in Mylapore next to the devotees in the Kapaaleshwar Temple. I see silk sarees, and I hear them rustle. I exchange glances with the demure and bear the stares of young boys with vibhuti on their forehead and oil in their hair. In the temple I gag at the ghee and oil and the roaches that roam in the dark chambers. I ply the aarti plate with small change and hold the prasadam carefully. I fall like a tree and press forehead to stone and I mumble a few lines of Sanskrit that someone planted in my head.

And I head to the Mylai Karpagambal Mess for more invocation and some hot food. I renew acquaintance with muzhaga podi and keerai vadai. And I am in the company of my relatives or at least those that look like my uncles and aunts. They are careful people who wash their hands before and gargle lustily after. Sambar comes in a bucket and vadai in a tray. Chutney makes splotches and runs. I am sitting on a bench next to three others. There is a fan overhead, a few lizards next to a light and one pesky boy with a runny nose who is being called 'Don't do this kanna'. I can make out this is an Iyer place.

At home the dread returns. I feel I am at a kutcheri, where a slow delineation of a raga is happening. Ragam

Tanam Pallavi. Make no mistake; this one will have a thani avarthanam. There will be a percussion duel.

* * *

The next time the bugger called I spoke in chaste Tamil. This was my attempt at a compromise. The fellows needed to know that I had my roots in this land. Balan hung up in confusion. 'Wrong number,' he mumbled before he disconnected.

That was the last we spoke. I had spotted two bikes parked near my house for three days in a row. One bike had a dented fender and a familiar colour. The riders I could not see. They would have staked themselves. Something would give very soon. In the meantime I walked up to their bikes, looked around pointedly and got to work. I deflated their tyres and filled sand in the fuel tanks. And I imagined them watching and laughter escaped me.

* * *

In a Chennai thundershower the thunder starts much before the cloud bank builds. There are layers of grey gloom; the skies have darkened today at 5 p.m. itself. The sound rolls in. The howl of the wind is followed by a crashing sound that splits the skies.

It is a Sunday. The bells begin to ring in the New Life Church in Saidapet. The churchman's din grows louder and louder. The pastor is a wild man. He has no face; just a mass of muscle rippling and striking the gong. His back is oiled like a thief of the night.

I am brought to my knees near the Saidapet bridge. At the base of my head lies the truth. Let the music play. I will not shiver. This is an honest mistake.

I can hear them call my name.

'Kumar?'

It is a voice from the past.

'Kumar, what have you done?'

I laugh. The wind carries my laughter and exuberant nature subsides. I get a pause. I hear the sound of running feet. Balan's friends gather. I face them. Balan lies at my feet.

The sound of a scythe; a descending blow.

Thrash the earth where my pieces lie.

LANGDA

I SAW A MAN TODAY. He looked fragile. I can think of no other word to describe him.

What does fragile look like?

He was hugging himself.

When I see images of the Egyptian Pharaohs lying with their hands folded, I feel they are protecting themselves from just the kind of leering that tourists engage in.

I am staring at this man like a tourist.

He is standing in the small porch in front of his small house in Rainbow Colony.

He looks salaried.

His clothes are discounted. His shirt is not tucked in and is a size too large. It droops over his shoulders. His pant is not ironed. His sandals have been repaired; some stitches are coming off.

He has a shock of hair that is almost fully grey.

His spectacles have a dark plastic frame and thick clear glasses.

He has no purpose. It is a working day and at this time his office will be working.

I imagine a tic in his left eye and a twitch in his left hand.

He looks so calm otherwise.

There is no doubt in my mind. I can see what will happen to him.

Left to himself he will come to grief.

From here on things will worsen.

I could change his life. I really could.

It is up to me.

The thing is I walked away.

I had nothing important to do that day. I could very easily have gone up to him and spoken.

* * *

I was distracted that whole day. At home and at work I was irritable and impatient.

The same thought plagued me. What would happen to him?

'Was there a commotion?' I ask the wife that evening.

She holds up her fingers and counts.

'A dog bit a man in the ankle, a pedigree dog. The cat has given birth to six kittens. Our driver has suspected typhoid and the milk van broke down in the middle of the road.'

'I meant in Rainbow Colony.'

That place was a street away from home.

'How would I know?' She shrugs.

The next day I had to travel. A new city took me away. I

returned after three days with a calm mind. I was absorbed in a new project.

* * *

I walked past that same house again. The porch was still there.

I paused in my stride and slowed down.

There were no signs. Nothing moved.

I feared the worst.

The curtains looked dirty. The entrance had no kolam. There was a light fixture without a bulb.

There were telltale signs that only I could see. They told me it wasn't too late.

The small gate had no lock and the latch could be opened from the outside.

And yet I walked away.

* * *

'What is your connection to the city?' asks my uncle Guptaji. He is looking at horoscopes of people he has not met. He will be deciding their fate.

'Connection?'

'Sambandh. You are a North Indian baniya, that is why I ask. Were you born here?'

'No, you know that. But I did all my schooling here.'

One horoscope catches his attention. He looks grimly at it. He crumples it and throws it accurately into a cane bin in a corner. 'Basket case,' he says. I cannot make out if he is trying to be funny. He examines another horoscope and his eyes glint. He shows it to me. It has a photograph of a girl; a good-looking girl. 'Vanity case,' says Guptaji. This time he laughs. He places it to a side and looks at me.

'You worked for so many years in Mumbai. And you travelled all over the world after that, like a madman trying to get lost.'

'Yes, and for some reason I came back to Chennai.'

'Yes. That is why I ask "What is your connection?" Why did you return?'

I thought this was a meaningless question. But this uncle of mine was not known for idle chatter.

'You mean to say it is in my horoscope?'

I should never have let him loose on my mine. The thought that something is pre-ordained is scary.

* * *

My feet take me to Rainbow Colony, to that street.

And I walk past that house for no reason.

What is my connection?

The house is locked. The gate has a padlock.

'Does somebody live here?' I ask the next-door neighbour.

I am whispering and looking very suspicious.

The reply is a whisper. I tiptoe away.

'You mean an old woman was inside the house?' asks the wife.

'Yes, and the door and the gate are locked when the husband goes away.'

'Why?'

'The woman is mad. She is dangerous mad. She has a self-preservation instinct that is triggered when she sees strangers.'

I changed my walking route and kept clear of that street.

But there were telltale signs that were unresolved.

* * *

I go for an after-dinner stroll. I haven't done this in ages.

And I go past that house. The frontage is dark but two rooms are dimly lit.

I see her. She is tall. Through the darkness I feel her piercing gaze.

'How do you know she saw you?' asks the wife.

'She was facing the road and I got goose bumps,' I reply. 'I never get goosebumps.'

'That's it?'

'Yes. Is it not enough?'

'Why did you go there? Why did you go for a walk in the night? What are you trying to prove?'

'I don't know. What should I do? For some reason I keep walking that way.'

'Either you stop going there or you go up and ring the bell.'

'When were you born, Kumar?'

'First day of March, first year of the sixties.'

'I know that,' replies Guptaji. 'I want to know what time?'

'7.30 in the morning. Why?'

My uncle is a strange fellow. He is part astrologer and part shaman.

'The day you were born a tree fell,' he says.

'Did it have roots?' I ask.

He looks startled. 'That is what my wife asked me then. She asked me the exact same question.'

'Did it?' I persist.

'It left a gaping hole in the ground.'

'Was it raining?' I ask.

'Yes,' he replies. His eyebrows are up by now. 'How do you know?'

'Was it a mango tree?' I ask for some reason.

And he nods and then he shakes his head, surprised at my questions.

I could have told him that it was a langda breed mango tree that grew from a thrown seed and like its name it turned out lame and never bore the fruit it was famous for. It never set roots as it was meant to coming as it did from north of the Vindhyas. And how did I know of all this? I had no idea.

I never saw that fragile man again. That man went away. His wife, his deranged wife left with him. I have no idea where they went. But strange inklings kept writing messages in my head and whenever I walked past that place things happened. It was becoming a nuisance. I was obsessed with that place. There was disquiet if I did not go down that road. There was an urge to walk in and confront something. The place was under lock and key and it was getting overrun with creepers and bushes.

* * *

Finally, I pick up courage to knock at the neighbour's door and enquire.

'That couple has a sad story,' says the neighbour. He is an old man himself and is happy to have someone to talk to.

'Why sad?' I ask.

'They lost their daughter when she was very young. Did you know?'

'No sir,' I reply. 'I have no idea.'

'Would you like to sit down?'

I sit on the edge of a mooda; a rope seat that prickles. The old man fusses around me and then warms up.

'It was an unexplained thing. The infant was just three

or four months old. It was one of those sleeping deaths, the kind that happens suddenly and by accident. The child was sleeping and unattended because it was raining very hard. So hard that water had collected all over the city and trees were falling, especially coconut trees. One tree, a large mango tree, fell into their compound and they were distracted for a couple of hours. The traffic was blocked and everybody was blowing the horn. But all was quiet in the child's room, so quiet that the mother ran. She picked up her daughter and...'

The man chokes and fights back tears.

'The doctors said there was no explanation,' he whispers. 'And the husband I think was hard on the wife.'

'Sudden Infant Death Syndrome,' I mumble.

'What sir?' asks the old man, leaning towards me.

'Nothing,' I reply. 'Were you there at the time it happened?'

He nods with a faraway look.

'It was so long ago but I remember it so clearly. I have held that infant in my arms. She had that baby smell of soap and powder.'

I shift around on that mooda while he relives his memories.

'I had gifted that girl an amulet even. Such a lovely young couple they were. And the child was so beautiful.'

'So the wife took it hard?' I ask after a while.

'She lost it. She was never the same again. She was convinced by her husband that she was responsible. She withdrew into her own world and never emerged. She used to have fits of rage and days of weeping. They became a strange couple. You know the husband used to lock the door and gate at all times when he went away? He never trusted his wife again.'

After this I should have let things rest but it was not in my hands. I still went down that road. I still walked past that gate. I regretted more than ever not having spoken to that fragile person. Finally one piece of the puzzle made me call Guptaji. I called my uncle the shaman.

I asked him a question that nagged me. 'Why did you enquire about my time of birth?'

He smiled.

'What is there to say?' he said.

'Why did you ask me my time of birth?' I repeated. 'Were you making my horoscope?'

'Answer this question first: did you meet that man finally?' he asked in return.

I shook my head with a tinge of regret.

'You should have,' said the shaman.

'Why?'

'Because he was waiting for you,' he replied.

I did a double take. Guptaji was not joking.

'What do you mean waiting for me? He did not know me at all.'

He was so irritating sometimes.

'These things happen for a reason, young Kumar. You see you were born on the day a storm happened in Chennai, on a day when a mango tree fell and at the very moment their daughter died.'

I was getting goose bumps again.

'You were meant to go up and meet him,' said Guptaji. 'While you were looking at him he was waiting to receive you. He would have taken you to meet his wife.'

II

THE VAGABOND

RANGASWAMY
I.I.T. Madras

'I AM RANGASWAMY, AN ENGINEER. I am a Mechanical Engineer from the Indian Institute of Technology, Madras. I graduated in the top three percentile at a time when Mechanical was the preferred branch of engineering and Madras was the IIT to go to for this discipline. I was never disciplined.'

'Stick to the facts,' said Senior Inspector Murthy. 'No need to be descriptive.'

The place was like a cauldron and it was just 10 a.m. Murthy looked like a pot on fire. Sweat was streaming down his cheeks and his hair had matted into black rivulets.

'Things happen to people who spend 4-5 years in an IIT,' continued Ranga, as if he hadn't heard. 'If you come from a Brahmin background like I did, then the sense of freedom you experience can turn your nights into days. I had my first drink in hostel. Smoking was part of high school but taking that further occurred to me in the midst of exams.'

'You are aware I am writing all this down?'

The record book looked like a ledger, the pen was a fountain pen and Murthy came from the old guard that could read their own handwriting.

'Classes were a necessary evil. I spent most of my time in my hostel, escaping now and then to acquire rum from a nearby TASMAC shop, a place that smelt of sweat and piss, that gave water in plastic sachets, that had the basics like brandy and whisky and did brisk business at 10 in the morning when the labour and the vocational class landed up for a quarter to help them through their day.'

'Again you are straying,' warned the Inspector.

'Open the bloody windows,' he shouted at the constable. 'Bloody fan,' he muttered. The sound of worn bearings was an irritant.

'I drank but I was not a drunk. I preferred weed. I needed time every week to tend to my weeds. I grew weed in a small obscure plot near the campus in Indiranagar. The owner had gone overseas and left a board that said NO TRESPASSING. I was a trespasser then. I think that has stuck with me more than anything else.'

The Inspector paused and took another look at the young man. An IIT engineer should have more sense than to babble like this. He decided to record selectively till such time as he made up his mind.

'What do you do now, I say?'

'Today I run Ranga Travels. It is a sole proprietorship. For me time is travel and travel is trespass and tourist guides are no more than tramps who cover ground that speaks out of history books. I read a lot of history and when I encounter terrain I am conscious of those that have been there before me and events that have taken place in these monuments and ruins.'

Senior Inspector Murthy was open-mouthed. This monologue has come from nowhere in this Police Station of his where, on a normal day, he recorded the scanty details of bums and thieves.

'You are talking to me as if I am a tourist. This is not a historical monument and I am not Veerapandiakattabomman; this is a police station.'

Ranga was still under the influence. He had been dragged into this cop station late at night. The binge that had started the previous evening had addled his brain. He had no recollection of how he had got here. Inside the lockup he had felt someone search his pockets and one drunk had felt his arse. Right now he was saying the first thing that came to mind.

'History is a sham, sir. Common men of valour are eulogized. Looters and plunderers become heroes. Nobody kept count of the numbers that were killed. No record was kept of their names. The history of this country is an amateur guide to events that took place. Myth and story fill the gaps between moth-eaten documents that have survived.'

Inspector Murthy had had enough. He stood him up and took him to the toilet. He emptied a bucket of water over his head and made him lean over the basin. Most of Ranga's dinner came out as did some bile.

'Retched life,' muttered Ranga. 'Why am I here and who are these people?'

These people were policemen who looked at him like he was about to run away. Last night he had fled when the police had arrived. He had vaulted over the railing in the middle of Sardar Patel Road and run into Anna University with a posse of bellied and bellicose cops straining to keep up. The mistake he had made was trying to climb a tree, a coconut tree.

Ranga sat in a corner and recovered. His pulse thudded in his head and his stomach rumbled audibly. He could feel his bloodshot eyes. Later the Inspector called him in and took down all his personal details and made him sign in the register.

'What do you actually do, Rangaswamy?' he asked for the nth time.

'Ranga Travels is a personal service,' parroted Ranga. 'We handle small groups, most often just one person and usually a female traveller.'

The good cop routine was on. 'Is it doing well?' asked Murthy, a little solicitously.

'I am a poor businessman,' said Ranga. 'And I have no succession plan,' he added.

'Anything else?' asked the Inspector. Every reply from this man was a surprise.

Ranga nodded. There was one question that was bothering him. 'By the way, have you heard of Woodstock?' he asked.

The good cop exploded. 'Bloody half-baked pappan fellow, I know who your father and mother are. Look at you; you sozzled and drugged-out Western civilization flunky. What a shame!'

'Why am I here?" asked Ranga. It occurred to him now that his presence at this place was unexplained.

'You are here on a rape charge,' said Murthy.

The words took some time to sink in. The bloody hangover lifted and landed with a thud.

'Rape?' said Ranga. 'Sex?' he queried. 'Last night?'

'Two days ago,' said Murthy, a little apologetically. He had not understood why the girl had taken so long to file a complaint. But she had brought evidence. Torn clothes, remnants of bruises, Ranga's personal effects; basically enough material to file an FIR and get this fellow in.

'You are sounding very disjointed,' said Inspector Murthy.

'Yes,' said Ranga. 'That is correct.'

He looked around the police station for concrete evidence that this was actually happening. A lady cop standing at the door frowned at him and turned away. Which reminded him.

'What was the girl's name?' asked Ranga.

* * *

She was five feet eight inches high. She wore no heels.

She was fulsome. But she wasn't wearing black.

She had long hair tied in a bun. There was no mascara.

She was trying to be jolly. In a way she was fun.

She arrives at the buffet table.

'Where is the curd?'

Her gait is an angular advance. She cannot set foot straight. The party is winding down and she has had one too many.

The curd has been set in a circular bowl and is placed at the far end of the buffet. I stand there waiting; knowing that from here to the exit is a short throw.

She spots my shoes. And that gives her an opening.

'Why are they called sneakers?'

I don't know.

'Young people wear them.'

I get it, lady.

'I have seen them in purple, red, green; you name the colour. Are they not tennis shoes?'

I look at my grey Converse version. I am the only one in the room wearing sneakers. My jeans have a small, deliberate tear and the edges have been stitched. I have raised eyebrows today. People who see me drink and people who see me smoke think I will never grow up. It helps them that I have a Yezdi bike, a tug-worthy beard and wide eyes.

'Where are you put up?' asks Jolly. She has a bowl of curd in her hands.

'I am a tenant in Rainbow Colony.'

'Oh I see, a tenant.' She sees a canapé in range. 'Vegetarian?' she asks the boy carrying the tray.

It is an ugly canapé; a piece of white cheese sitting on top of a canned pineapple tukda. A plump cherry is impaled atop the cheese.

'Who is your landlord?'

'I have not met him.'

The curd distracts her. It is pearly white and has been set well. Every spoonful breaks fresh, creamy ground and there is no whey left behind.

'I must be going,' she says finally. She doesn't.

What am I doing? I mean this is Friday evening and I am stuck with Rambo Jolly and small talk.

'Were you pretty once?' I ask.

As a pick-up line I have done better but I also know that to tell a good-looking girl that she is so, is to state the obvious. I am not a rude person and certainly not to women. Luckily this girl laughed and she laughed so loudly that I had to shush her up and we left the place in a hurry.

This was the beginning. This was the beginning of this end.

* * *

She is once divorced and far removed from the reality that has set in since.

She likes her cocktails spiced. Make that spiked.

Her clothing sense is disarray. What is tied will loosen, what is loose will flow.

The thirties are a time for renewal. You can ask me.

'My husband...' she begins.

'Distant memory, bad recall.'

She laughs. She holds the stem of her glass, twirls the contents and looks at me.

'My marriage...' she resumes.

'An experiment that ran aground.'

She holds her ground. Just about.

'What are you?'

How should I say this?

'I am a habit you do not need.'

She gathers wits. She traces her name in the sand.

L A I L A

Out in the open the sea breeze blows and the sound of waves are a constant refrain.

'What happens now?' she slurs. 'I need a travel advisory.'

And she giggles.

I am stoking fire. There is meat on the spit and tequila on ice.

'Did you marinate?' she asks.

I bring out the massage oil. She drains her drink and traces the rim of her glass down her throat.

'Did you tell me your name?' she teases.

I am done with her neck and shoulders. 'This is so good,' she says. Her skin is alabaster marred by a tracery of needle marks that form sinister tattoos on her arms. 'This is sooo good,' she says, giving in, yielding.

The sand is wet in my hair, in my face. I am lost amongst limbs. This is so fucking good. She calls me names, many names from an 'Order of Men', from a well travelled society. It hurts to hear the names of others.

* * *

'You can know a person in a weekend. All you need to know. Don't sleep a wink. Don't force anything. Just be alive.'

It is a cheap motel. The towels have brown specks that were once red. The floor has sand.

We walk around Mahabalipuram. We buy raw mango pieces and peanut pods. There is gooseberry to squeak our teeth.

A guide sidles up with his breath of rum.

'You are perfect picture,' he purrs.

I find a cigarette that is loosely packed. It lights up in a high flame.

I take photographs of her with settings, amongst old women with discoloured teeth, amongst old men sitting on their haunches and amongst children and their whimsy.

'You have to be lucky,' says she.

'Sorry?'

'To know somebody truly, you have to be lucky.'

I had lost the thread. Her mind moves on twin tracks.

A vendor of coloured drinks wheels by. I choose a dark colour with lime and ice.

'Don't trust what you are having,' she says. 'Don't catch something I don't need.'

48 hours. We caught ourselves falling. We rescued each other from drowning. There is a dark country beyond reason. It envelops you and takes you where it is hard to breathe.

Long nights, just two of them, each took me to a loam, to a shoreline where the sea never showed. There was liquid rock and hope. There was violence too somewhere in the mix. Some things did not feel right.

Monday morning has a different dawn. I have a few things and a duffel bag but I cannot pack well. I have a few bruises too.

'Will you say goodbye?' she pleads.

I am supposed to be good at this.

I say my goodbyes. I mean it, I insist. Who am I fooling?

I found her that weekend. It was a place I wanted to be. I cannot believe she went away and never looked back.

* * *

Inspector Murthy leaves Ranga in custody and proceeds to another location where a man had lost his belief and killed himself. Or so it seemed. This phrase hung around Murthy's life like the gold chain around his neck. Everything in his life was layered and it was for him to dig deep below the circumstantial and the evident till he reached the basest emotions that men and women have. Most people were normal; or so it seemed, till Murthy cast his eagle eye.

In the jeep he considered what he had seen of Ranga and while drugs can induce you to do strange things the essential nature of people was what interested him. This Ranga was not all that bad. He was misguided, perhaps lost; or so it seemed. Another session with him was required. Yes, just one would do.

* * *

The lockup at Adyar Police Station felt unclean. Ranga examined himself, saw his dirty nails, his soiled shirt sleeves and smelt his ambient smell. He felt like puking again. 'Where the fuck am I?' had been answered. 'What the fuck am I?' seemed a better question. A few of his friends had come and gone after making some tender enquiries but the press was beginning to sniff around. There was a low rumble outside as this case was getting noticed.

Clarity was what he needed. What the fuck had happened? The problem was he knew, he knew it the moment the accusation was made.

There was a girl, yes, one of many but this one was strange.

* * *

'I am going to have to throw you to the wolves,' said Inspector Murthy. 'You're not saying anything and it is going to hurt you.'

His station was bursting at the seams. He looked hassled. A German tourist had filed this rape complaint and she was tall and good-looking and she was making no attempt to protect her privacy. This was the worst-case scenario; a rape victim in the public eye. This boy Ranga would be quartered and hung.

'It was consensual,' blurted Ranga.

The Inspector laughed. This was hackneyed, stupid even, and an insult to his long years of service.

'I am a man of the world,' he said sagely. 'I know what consensual sex looks like.'

Ranga did not know how to put it but he had to say it. 'It was consensual rape,' he said.

To lessen the absurdity he had to add something. 'It was play-acting.'

And then Ranga reached out, held the Inspector's hands and broke down. Murthy was embarrassed. This Casanova suddenly looked like a child and this episode was beginning to look like a television soap.

'Sir, you have to believe me, she made me do all this. It looks bad, but believe me, we did this the way she wanted.'

Ranga remembered the night as a drugfest. He had a faint recollection of his forcing his way on her, something that did not appeal to him. She feigned resistance and induced pursuit. She gave in with great difficulty, behaving like a hellcat and victim till the very end. He had lain back exhausted and curiously spent. She had taken him in her arms, spoken to him softly as if to an errant child and they had done it again, this time with a tenderness that he had never seen, ever.

Laila had churned his insides and played havoc with him. He was totally fucked up.

Inspector Murthy was confused. He had raided the girl's den and discovered a rich stash of drugs and some pornographic material. A medical examination had revealed needle marks in her arms as well.

'How long were the two of you together?' asked the Inspector.

Ranga thought hard about places and dates. 'I cannot recollect exactly,' he said.

His honesty worked in his favour.

'Why would she file this charge if you were having a good time? Did you ditch her or something?'

'No,' said Ranga. 'I have no idea.'

Inspector Murthy had some idea. Ranga and the girl had been together for a week. That was hardly a background for a rape. Second, the girl was clearly hallucinatory.

'I could not handle her,' mumbled Ranga. That was some confession.

Right now even Murthy could not handle the girl. She was in withdrawal, remission or whatever the denial of drugs to an addict was called. The girl had shouted and screamed and was sitting in a corner, shivering. Two constables stood nearby and looked at her in awe.

Murthy wanted her in a hospital and out of his hands. He had an ace up his sleeve: the girl's expired visa. Time to wrap up.

'Are you a tourist guide or a gigolo?' he asked Ranga.

'I don't know,' was the reply. 'I am just a guide for the willing.'

* * *

Laila returned a year later. She kept calling till I relented and took her call. She was off drugs and had been through rehab.

'Why are you calling me?' I asked her. 'I am somebody you need to forget.'

She said that she needed to lay my ghost to rest; for both of us.

She came and she looked as stunning as before.

We drove around the country in my jeep for a whole week. We never touched, not once. She sat beside me and occasionally I flirted with her hair as it blew my way. Occasionally I felt where her hand had been. And once in a while I sat where her fragrance had taken hold.

She made me guide her through history and monument.

She made me do my job by the letter. This was new. I was finding new ground.

All the time she had eyes only for me. She saw through them.

I found an incurable romantic inside me. Denial honed its shape. Distance built its fervour.

All my previous flings landed and crashed. Proximity is a crumbly substance, I learnt.

'Can you do more than just guide?' she asked. 'You have such a reputation.'

'Look at her eyes now and see them laugh,' I said to myself.

I handed her the travel documents across the railing. Her boarding call had just been announced. I could not look her in the eye.

She placed her hand on mine. The first touch at parting.

'Have I missed something?' she teased.

She had me there. I was truly taken.

* * *

Ranga Travels continues. For some days I was reviled, shunned and in a hard place, alone. There wasn't much to ponder. I was off substances for good. Well, maybe the odd joint now and then.

These days I carry road films in my head.

I listen to string music from *The Motorcycle Diaries*.

I find Wim Wenders when I hold a camera. His narratives plague my mind.

Curiously I still feel I haven't grown up yet.

RANGASWAMY, BETROTHAL

'Why do we meet so often?' I ask.

The question was not meant to hurt. An answer was not expected either.

'We are not even related,' I blurt.

He looks hurt at the reminder.

'Why say it?'

We drink two; the first a measured large, the second an approximate. There is a bond that develops after the second.

'We have a common wall,' says Ranga. 'That counts for something.'

We look down at it. It has crumbled around the middle.

'And it is a low one too,' I reply.

This was a dangling conversation, one that begged for wind.

The third drink was a strain that day. It was forced. The fourth went down well.

'You want to tell me something?' he says finally.

People want to say things to Rangaswamy. He knows it.

'You are a failed romantic,' I tell him. 'You exist because of rock n' roll, because of Ginsberg's poetry and the one truly beat generation he came from.'

He drinks to that, looks pleased and quotes from 'An Eastern Ballad'.

I have become another child

I wake to see the world go wild.

We drink to that too.

Ranga's eyes have narrowed and he is smoking so I cannot make out if he is expressionless. He usually is. But he did say this.

'I disagree with the first part of what you said; I am not a failed romantic. Haven't you heard; flagrant love can be fragrant.'

That night we went to the terrace and stood on a nine-inch wall and spread our arms to test the wind. It was still. We took two steps each to test our lives. I think we fell.

* * *

Ranga had an uncle who was a regular bandicoot, a peruchaali, a low-slung creature, alert to low-life. In the family lounge there was no space for him on pedestal or trophy wall. He was the anointed pariah.

'He is a womanizer, I say,' said the elders. 'And a drunk,' added the rest.

It had reached a stage where he couldn't shock them anymore. Fellow was called Balu.

Balu had a technician's brain, a high IQ and a complete lack of industry. In school he discovered an adeptness at trigonometry that matched his comfort with calculus. He discovered tobacco too. He became cocky and confident; after all, he had gifts from the Gods. In college these gifts found no expression beyond writing equations when dead drunk. Mornings he could be found climbing a ladder or descending a staircase on his cycle. He looked unkempt.

Balu wore dark glasses at night. Age had not been kind on eyes touched by the clap. His visits to the brothels were always unprotected. Where was the time? When a coughing fit threw up blood he went to the doctor. The doctor read him a list of don'ts, saw the expression on his face and then tore it up.

'You have no time, Balu. Pass on your mantle,' he said.

So Balu the Rake called Ranga the Nephew.

'Enough of your wild ways, thambi. There cannot be two of us in the same family digging our graves.'

It was a feeble attempt.

'Settle down, bugger,' said Balu, a little gruffly. 'Otherwise you will end up like me.'

'Who will marry a history-sheeter like me?' asked Ranga; a fair question.

Bala snorted. 'That is done with. Everyone knows it was a bad episode and while you were smelling of manure and not roses, at the end of it you are not what that woman claimed you to be.'

'The memory that rankles never goes away,' said Ranga, speaking for himself.

'People who forget have done nothing,' replied Balu, sounding confused as ever.

They pondered their equilibrium.

'But you did reconcile, I hear?' said Balu. Ranga nodded. 'So find a girl and settle down,' ordered his uncle.

Ranga indulged him.

'Balan Sir, find me a Punjabi and I will settle down,' he said. 'Find me a full-cream from Mother Dairy.'

* * *

Ranga had known a Punjabi girl; one young thing in bloom. It was a brief dalliance. She had come down from Delhi for some study. It was her first time south of the Dravidian line. She was amazed at his fair complexion, his English diction and his ways.

'You are not a Tamilian, cannot be.'

She had amazing skin, amazing teeth and amazing hormones.

He continued to surprise her.

In the midst of a romp she shrieked, 'I thought you would be a vegetarian.'

He was.

She had a view on life that was myopic. Everything beyond the next week was blurred. She asked Ranga for nothing. He realized that after she had left. Yet she left him bereft and he went to his uncle and rambled. They smoked a few cigarettes till Balu coughed.

'What did she take away?' asked Balu. 'You have nothing to give.'

Ranga looked confused.

'I mean, why do these things happen? For no reason?'

Balu blew some more smoke. 'Life is a puzzle,' he said. 'Don't make too much of it. It will sort itself out.'

* * *

'I have called Athimber,' I inform him.

'Why him?' asks Ranga.

'Because none of the women in the family want to be involved with your betrothal.'

Ranga looks surprised but when he thinks about it, reason dawns.

'Why Athimber? He is such a dodo.'

I explain patiently.

'He is a match-maker in our circles. He has a keen eye for matrimony. Plus he has the bank account details of everybody so all reference checks begin and end with him. He knows every deposit and every withdrawal and of course he knows the fixed deposit balance as well.'

'So he will have seen my account?'

Ranga thinks about the prospect. Most of his payments came in cash and some were in foreign currency. It would look very suspicious.

'I will be rude at the first meeting,' he warns.

That was fine, all bachelors who got dragged to the wedding hall started rude. Most ended up resigned after a while.

* * *

Athimber has been prepared for the meeting. He has been given the gory details. He comes expecting a savage but finds a friendly gorilla. They chat for a while about inanities and Ranga is quite funny. Athimber begins to like him, which is strange.

'Am I your biggest challenge?' asks Ranga.

'Because of your record?' asks Athimber.

Ranga nods.

Athimber shakes his head vigorously.

'On the contrary, you are easy to place. You belong to a very small group of people who are hard to slot. The thing is this group has nowhere to go and you have only each other.'

Ranga laughs till tears flow down his cheeks.

'We will see about that,' he says finally. 'You may begin.'

'What are you looking for, Ranga?' begins Athimber.

As a general question it begged a long answer.

'No divorcee,' starts Ranga.

'Of course,' agrees Athimber. There went half the database.

'And no amputee.'

'You don't have to be offensive,' says Athimber.

The fight began there.

Ranga wants a shortlist of none and he gets there very quickly.

'I am done with sex,' says Ranga. 'You must inform them. I am tired and down for the count.'

We all laugh.

'What about rum?' asks the unflappable Athimber.

Matters improve thereafter.

* * *

A proposal came delivered by hand in an unmarked cover. The address was written by hand, by a good hand. The envelope had no scent, so nothing cheap. Inside was one foolscap sheet and it had scant detail. But it was forceful enough for Athimber to sit up and adjust his spectacles. He went to Balu who looked at it and smiled.

'He has met his match,' he said.

Ranga got a routine call and he came late as was his wont. He wore no finery. The misfiring of his Yezdi bike woke up the neighbourhood. Ahead of him came the twin exhausts of rum and tobacco.

Rum got served, small shots in small tumblers and no fanfare to dilute its strength. The two elders looked on as Ranga tried to make himself comfortable.

'There is one who is willing; no questions asked.'

The questions came thick and fast.

'Does she know about me?'

'Yes.'

'I mean, really know about me?'

'She knew some and we told her some.'

'Does she smoke?'

'No.'

'Does she drink?'

'Yes.'

'Never been married?'

'No.'

The pause happened because they had not reached this far before.

'Can I see her details, a photograph?'

He stretched out his hand.

'No. She has this as a condition. No photographs.'

Ranga looked at both of them. They were not smiling and they were not known to waste time.

'I have never heard of a blind-date marriage,' he told them.

'She said if she met you socially, it would not happen.'

Ranga was intrigued.

'What if I say yes? What is the guarantee that I will go through with this? So why go through this charade?'

'We don't have all the answers. But these are the conditions. Is it yes or no?'

'Obviously a no. I am not short of company as you will know.'

Then came the emotional card.

'Balu wants you to do it. He says this is a match.'

Ranga could not believe this was happening. He needed a clue. He ran through a few.

'Does she write her name in sand? Does she want to go but never leaves? Does she ask for a heartfelt goodbye? Or is she just a tease?'

'Which one should I answer first?' said Athimber. And then he told him what she had said. 'She asked me to tell you that you had a mole in two parts. In Hindi she said it was a gaal ka thil.'

Ranga started to smile. He had no mole on his cheek but there were other places where cheeks did meet.

* * *

Athimber and I sit after Ranga has gone.

'Tell me more about this girl.'

He spreads his arms helplessly.

'There isn't much. I sent the details on Ranga and this girl got back immediately. I spoke to her and I was convinced. I had to meet her.'

'You've met her already?'

He nods.

'What a girl she is,' he recounts in wonder.

'Easy Athimber, easy.'

'I need a drink,' he says.

He gets one. He looks at it suspiciously and drinks it down fast like beginners do.

'Never in my life have I questioned myself like this.

People like Ranga and this girl make me question my life. They do strange things but they are nice people.'

I let him be for a while.

'You think this is a good match?' I ask.

'I don't know, this time I have no idea. The girl is like Ranga; same life, many men. She said that she and Ranga have spent a weekend together some years ago. The girl remembers. She is sure he wouldn't.'

'So why would she do it?'

'Exactly.'

'Why would he?' I ask.

'Exactly.'

'It might work,' I tell him. He looks askance.

'Haven't you heard? Flagrant love can be fragrant.' I quite like that line.

III

THE HOUSEWIFE

THE MONEYLENDER AND THE PRIEST

RAMDAS IS A MAN OF GOD and he feels that the one above is always watching. When he writes his innermost thoughts he looks around surreptitiously and hides the page with his hands. He takes a pencil and licks the lead. Poison has no taste.

He writes in the early hours of the day. Moonlight does things to him.

He starts with capitals. 'MOUNAM.'

He needs to add something to that.

'I am an apprentice of silence.'

No further thoughts come to his head. He drags the pencil and the words come out like doodles.

The next day he hounds people. He is a bad ass who is short of sleep.

'Ramdas, go live alone,' they tell him.

'But I do,' he protests. 'And I do not like it.'

Nobody shares his world.

His house has no gate. There are two unpainted cement pillars at the entrance and two hinges as well but there is no gate. People still stand outside and peep in. What they see looks uninviting. The house looks like a rummaged drawer. Clothes hang on window sills and door jambs. A tap drips endlessly and a half-painted cupboard teeters on a low bench.

Ramdas is a happy camper and that spirit invites strays. On the days he wakes up late the cats get his milk packet. And in the lazy afternoon when he sleeps in his rocking chair in the verandah, his small house front becomes a den for street dogs.

One day he is moved to confess. He sees his scooter, which hasn't started in the last two years and his cycle whose wheel chain has broken. Both have gathered dust.

'I am going nowhere,' he writes.

'Ram, you need a wake-up call,' says his neighbour.

'I need a rooster,' he replies. 'I need a cock that crows.'

'Have you seen the crows?' he is asked.

It is an issue. The cawing black birds circle and descend every day. They make a din in his front yard and they pin each other down. It could be an omen.

'What's with them?' thinks Ramdas. There is no food he spots, nor carrion that lies.

'It is an omen,' says his neighbour. 'You are a Brahmin, you know the portent.'

Ramdas looks for portent in his scriptures and ends up sneezing. They have gathered dust too.

'Praanam.

Life is a device,' he writes that night. 'It tells you time.'

He thinks of his day. It had been uneventful. The temple was closed for renovation, if you please. He picks a fresh page.

'Kaalam.

I used to count minutes. Now I count days.'

His doodles spread like ink.

Life changes when visitors come. Two men came with an attitude that smelt of roadside trickery. They had a forced air of humility and helpfulness. They left behind a form to be filled. It is marked 'URGENT'. Ramdas gives it respect by looking at it all day. The next day he is distracted. His digestion is in tatters after a meal at a wedding that he had conducted.

The bell rings and he is caught napping. He rubs his eyes. Who could be coming at this hour? He walks the corridor that leads from the kitchen to the verandah in front. The two young fellows stand with papers in their hand.

'You have come for the election roll?' he asks.

His name was not on the voter's list. He had been lazy. So there was that form to fill.

Their heads bob and the smiles ingratiate.

'Come tomorrow, I am busy.'

The smiles pause. 'Sir, it is difficult to come back.' At least they were honest.

'I am very slow at filling forms,' he tells them.

'Sir, leave the matter to us. We will fill the form,' says one hurriedly. 'You only have to come with us and sign.'

Ramdas has developed an acute dislike that he is finding hard to hide. His lips want to curl and his tongue has sharpened. A blurt is around the corner.

'Why don't you finish the rest of the street and come back,' he says.

They go away quietly. There is no door to slam.

Ramdas realizes he is cornered. He had avoided this form-filling for many elections and during the last census he had faked a serious illness. If people knew who he really was he would be banished from the temple.

He looks at the form in trepidation.

NAME:

Ramdas, he writes. Then he adds Samarth. And to make it honest he adds: 'My given name was Narayan.'

AGE:

Old. That sounded correct. There was no point in guessing a number. I was eight years old when my father died and he died when the British were leaving. I knew they were leaving because things stopped working for a week. There were no birth records in our village but there was a man who had palm leaves. He inscribed birth and death. One morning his house caught fire and he was a late riser. There is one reliable detail: I was born on Ram Navami.

NAME OF FATHER OR HUSBAND:

Father was called Suryaji.

FULL ADDRESS:

I have changed six houses. Currently I am at Rainbow Colony. It is the house without a gate.

IDENTIFICATION MARK:

After so many years my forehead bears marks and my fingertips have burnt. Coconut splinters have cut my legs.

RELIGION:

He writes hobby and then corrects it to profession. Neither sounded correct. I am a devout Hindu. Would there be less devout as a category? He could point many fingers at Rainbow Colony. The less devout filled his temple and his plate. When he was done with the aarti he would stand with a plate and the Colony would troop past. They would have eyes for the deity behind him and he would look at their eyes. What he saw made him despondent.

MARITAL LIFE:

My foster mother tried to get me married when I was twelve years old. I ran away before the ceremony could be completed. As I was leaving the pandal the pandit was saying 'Saavdhan'. I was very careful thereafter.

PROFESSION:

Temple Priest.

INCOME:

Middle, he wrote. He felt he should write it as 'Lower middle'.

He looked around at the room in which his pot called the kettle. He always wrote in his kitchen. There was a platform that stretched the length made of black, polished granite. He would stand next to the gas cylinder and sniff. He was afraid of leaks. He would test the knobs on the stove till the smell came. The knobs were shaky and stood between open and shut. He would wipe the counter with his thundu which hung from his right shoulder. And he would pull at the sacred thread till the knot settled where it didn't tickle. There was always paper and pen next to the masala box. The paper had tinges of haldi, red chilli powder and tea. It looked handmade.

Behind him was an old Kelvinator fridge. When the compressor came on it would shudder and whine. Inside the fridge was curd, fruit, vegetables in small measures and ground rice paste.

In the corner was a mortar and a pestle and a larger stone contraption for grinding rice.

Above it, next to a yellow bulb was a calendar that marked all the kalams, the festivals and the other holidays. There was a rendering of Murugan; quite angelic.

There was no microwave, no electric oven and no mixie.

He corrected the form to Lower middle.

He signed the form with a flourish and handed it over when the persistent fellows came again. He was to go the next day to the office to sign the register.

When he landed up at the office they were waiting for him. The officer looked at him closely and then shot up and bowed. He recognized him as the pandit at the temple, the pujari. And he had him seated and called for water and sherbet. And he enquired about his health and the progress of the temple renovation. After some minutes had passed Ramdas had had enough.

'Is there a problem with the form?' he asked.

The officer nodded. He asked for the two fellows to stand outside and then he spoke.

'There is a young, single girl who has also given a form. She lives a few streets away.'

He coughed delicately.

'It would seem she is your daughter.'

Having dropped this bombshell he pushed a photocopy of a filled form towards Ramdas. The latter read it carefully.

FATHER'S NAME: Samarth Ramdas, also called Narayan. He is a religious scholar and a yogi.

RELIGION: Deshastha Rugvedi Brahmin

PROFESSION: I am a religious scholar and yogi.

The address had been erased in the photocopy.

Ramdas blinked a few times. The officer was a little

apologetic. At the same time he had to resolve this mysterious coincidence. He pushed Ramdas's form towards him.

'Would you like to make any corrections?' he asked.

Ramdas came clean. 'Tear up the form. It is a pious fiction,' he replied.

'Pious?'

Ramdas dipped his fingers into his glass of water and sprinkled some drops on his form.

'Sant Ramdas exists, I have merely borrowed his mantle.'

The officer had moved on to the next form.

'Sir, can you be clearer?'

'I am a follower of the Sant. I was a scholar who pursued his life history. My real name is just Narayan.'

He was reluctant to divulge more as now he would have to unlock what was buried many long years.

'So these other details you have filled in are of the Sant?'

Ramdas nodded.

'Then how come this girl has also used the same details?'

The old man smiled ruefully and shrugged.

'Would you believe something because it is written? My study of the Scriptures was based on this question.'

'Can we do without riddles?' asked the officer. 'What should I believe?' He had a day's work ahead of him and these two forms were taking up his time.

'Here is the story,' said Ramdas finally. 'I am an uprooted Brahmin. I used to stay in Kumbakonam with my family. My wife...'

He choked and then gathered himself. His voice dropped.

'My wife had an affair with the local moneylender. I am sure of it. The fellow suddenly released all my pledged material. Why would he do that?'

The affair still rankled. He was surprised at the anger that has surfaced in him after all these years.

'We fought for nine months. Right through the pregnancy I gave my wife hell. I did not want that child to be born. But she still bore a daughter. I banished them from my life. The woman protested right till the end. She left and she cursed me as she went. My ears are still ringing with those curses.'

'Then?'

'I shifted to Madras and began a new life; a modest life, the life of a non-entity. Nobody knew where I came from. I am a priest, so nobody questions.'

Ramdas reached for the girl's form. He wanted to see the handwriting again.

'Why is the address erased?' he asked.

The officer shrugged.

'Sorry sir, I cannot allow that.'

The mystery was still a puzzle.

'So you are telling me that this girl is really your daughter and she has found you and she has been staying in your vicinity without your knowing?'

Ramdas nodded. 'It has to be her.'

'Why would she do this? Why would she follow your footsteps?'

Ramdas felt a tug somewhere. Could this be his flesh and blood?

'I honestly don't know,' he whispered. 'I don't know what to believe.'

This girl would have walked past his house. She would have come to the temple. She would have stood in line when he bought provisions at the Murugan Store.

'Children need to know,' said the officer. 'Children are curious about these things.'

He tapped his pencil on the table. Time up.

'So which form should I take as the truth?' he asked.

'Neither, I guess,' said Ramdas. 'Both are untrue. I am not a sant, neither is she.'

'But she could be your daughter. Would you like to meet her?' asked the officer.

He stamped both forms as verified and tossed them onto a heap. He knew the answer he would get.

ASYLUM

KAALAM

I CAME ALIVE WHEN I MISSED A PERIOD. The anticipation causes a funk, the extended waiting a blue funk. I had a calendar that was marked in red and the date came and went, the weekend came and went and I remember clearly a bird on a tree singing for rain, a squall on the horizon that was a tease and a careless bee in the house that buzzed till it fell. I heard two men who quarrelled outside about parking a car and I saw an ad on television that asked me to go out and prance in the rain because their pads could soak up and not leave a stain. It was a strange time to be feeling uplifted.

'Eat your egg,' said my mother.

I burst out laughing.

'What?'

'Nothing.'

It was a strange time to be eating eggs. In my room I waited and read about Immaculate Conception. And I watched films. A few days later I bled copiously.

'Eat your egg,' said my mother.

I wept copiously.

'Come here, let me feel your forehead.'

I let her touch me. Her touch was tender.

'Mrs Ramdas?'

My tone made her pause.

'Is my father a moneylender or was it the priest?'

The biological subtext plays in my mind. Is the moneylender a molester? Or is the priest a eunuch? And can I please choose a father who is neither? What kind of a man lets go of my mother? She is a good woman, a good model, a fine chassis, an honest housekeeper, a careful mother, a caring friend and if there are other virtues you seek you can go fuck yourself. If eyes could speak I would have sworn I had an answer to my question from my mother. She would never speak out in this lifetime. What did her eyes tell me? Fuck knows. Brother, sometimes that is all there is to it. Fuck only knows.

The day before I bleed I need a man between my legs. Preferably someone who performs and leaves without introducing himself. Such people should come and ring the bell. Not the others who arrive in my vicinity and look at me like I am a vendor of body parts. Looking is free brother but if you brush past it will cost you.

'Your father is a scholar,' replied my mother. 'He knows Sanskrit.'

It was said simply, not in defence. I wish she would say something really harsh about him some day. How else am I to learn, place my family in perspective, deal with demons in the shape of men and live with troubled thoughts of broken clichés and unfinished song?

I slept that afternoon. I slept badly, on my stomach, one toss to the left, one to the right, one stare at the ceiling and one beside. And then I dreamt a bad one, a senseless one, one that comes from a lunch that sat inside you seeking churn.

In my sleep I am a pot of cannibal soup. My feet are trotters, my flanks are well done and my head floats in a thalai curry. Next to me are bits and pieces of a cousin mired in a biryani. Men are waiting for my mother to garnish.

'The salt is wanting,' she says. Shc sprinkles.

I start groaning. The damn salt hurts. My father is at the door and they spot his kudumi. He wants to come in but they won't let him. This is not a place for Brahmins, they tell him. Finally he arrives to the sound of burps.

I awoke, distended and disoriented, felt my bloated stomach and descended to the kitchen. It was evening, my breath tasted foul and the aromas were muzhagu and jeeragam.

'Am I on the menu?' My mother looked at my eyes and then at my dishevelled shape.

'Don't say anything,' I told her.

I tasted the evening rasam. It was my mother's signature dish and in its subtle aromas and quick and simple presentation a metaphor too. The salt fought the puli, the perungayam meditated and the fiery muzhagu hoisted itself up and fluttered its standard. My mother looked askance.

'Needs some blood,' I quipped and fled.

* * *

Evenings in Chennai and the lights come on. The first light is the one at the entrance, the vasapadi, and I fold my hands in reflex like my forebears did. After that a light in every room is switched on at my insistence. Every room is a temple and each gets my aashirvadam.

I hate dark evenings, I hate dull lighting and I hate tube-lights. Most of our walls are a chandanam yellow or a pista green. In this fluorescence my mother sits and decorates herself. She bathes twice a day. After the dinner is cooked she has a hot bath and then she wears a full saree, brushes her hair, knots it and adorns it with flowers, applies a hint of kajal and a round of kumkumam, twists her nose ring and then her ear-rings, looking all this while at her mirror image that turns coy. She takes a touch of ash from an earlier aarti and blesses me and her mother; the forgotten living and the remembered dead. I sit and watch the world go by. In my eyes this is a reaffirmation of all that does not make sense, of what should not be happening because it has no formal purpose other than keeping yourself whole, together and in one piece.

I know the meaning of this life and I know this way to dusty death. I have an illustrious female legacy; of what, I do not know. It is not significant or meaningful. It is a life that is shadow. It is not life in the limelight, in the forefront, exposed with all edges tested, with strength to endure cavil and the ability to inflict on others the burden of your journey. Perhaps this is life without a meaningful male counterpoint. The absence of strife or adversity from male companionship has dealt a mortal blow. There is no feminist agenda, no protest; just a civil calm, a becalmed ordinariness.

This is a life where you lack a life form. This is a life where you finally take a life.

* * *

MADYANAM

I came to Cenotaph Road with my mother. She came to Chennai in search of her husband. The thought makes me cringe. This was the man who had sent her away. It was easy for her to find him. She had faith, she said her prayers every day and she went to every temple she came across. She went wearing dark glasses and her head was covered with her pallu. Her husband, who had left her on suspicion of an affair, was a temple priest. He was the head priest in a temple in Eldams Road. Once she saw him there she never went there again. She did inform me and placed no restriction on my meeting him if I wished to. My parents never met in Chennai but in a sense they lived in the vicinity and were still married. My mother never wore white.

My mother has never had an affair. I think. If she did I would know. Why am I sure? I am capable of things she would not dream of. So I know. She has rekhas she will not cross, I have Laxman.

She was a schoolteacher. Her means were modest. She came into an inheritance when her father passed away and she moved with her mother and me to Chennai where she bought a house on a slightly tony road with the English sounding name of Cenotaph. The house belonged more to the neighbouring Rainbow Colony in spirit and appearance. It was here that she spent her last years. She used to read. She used to read to spring-clean her mind.

She called me on nights when the weather hung heavy and in the dim light we would sit on her bed shielded by curtains and she would show me her treasure trove. This would be bits that she had pieced together, curated if you please. There were two printed scarves, one really old pendant, some heavy jewellery that showed its age by dimming its burnish, a letter she had received from a long-lost friend, a photograph of Mansur Ali Khan Pataudi in jodhpurs standing sideways and favouring an eye, a recipe for a daring sambar that had won an award, a dried flower from her first garden that had by now bleached and had veins to show, a book of limericks, a book with nonsense verse which she had annotated, two pens that looked precious, a small silver box that was carved painstakingly and had ash from Baba, a small calendar print of Murugan which according to her had an imperfection, a page on which she had written Hey Ram a hundred times and this sheet had taken hues from pujas over the years, a prescription written by a doctor friend that had given her a rash and the medicine was subsequently banned, a small playful Krishna, a plain gold ring, a studded bracelet, a heavy waistband made of gold that I tried to hide afraid that robbers would catch the glint, an amulet from her childhood, a jewelled hair clasp and finally amidst all this some space for me to sit.

'Why are you doing this?' This was my unasked question.

'Is this what I will become?'

Make some distance, Sandhya, peel away and look; what do you see?

I see her walls. They have pictures of gods in colour. And they have black and white photographs of her near and dear who have passed on. The photography collection started with her parents and soon two sisters joined them and then a favourite uncle and finally her brother who was estranged and yet was given place once he had truly departed. These framed prints wore garlands of dry flowers, dull beads and on certain days a fresh mala would be placed and a few tears would be shed.

There was the wall and there was the bed and for me the litany was on the bed even if the remembrance was on the wall. The walls sang a dirge and the bed was a wake. And I was a wreck. I had to dig deep to free myself from this labyrinth where dwelled an unease. My mother was a source of a strange unease. She invoked in me a curious dread. Around her were all the clichés and few surprises. The only surprise sitting there was me.

Who the fuck is a housewife? If that is an occupation what does she occupy? Will I step into this role and essay it? As a housewife I will belong to a house like a lunatic belongs to an asylum, with good reason to escape and no will to surrender.

* * *

I live in a country that deals in entitlements. Strange as that sounds, entitlements are barter in our good land we call India. Free electricity is a line tap away. If you grow crops you pay no tax. The animal called subsidy grows in size every year, eating from the common pool that has grown but lost its accounts. Our maidservant disappears on days the free distributions happen. Around election time and after the results were announced she used to get free rice, a saree and a veshti. Then came a cooker, a wet grinder and a television. On the anvil is a laptop.

I do not grudge her any. I just want mine. I am a voter too. I want eyes that are not so close to each other. I want skin a shade lighter, hair a shade darker, six additional inches of height and four inches around the chest.

When I see my mother I am pained. She is beautiful. Honestly, she is good-looking. She has the best of complexion and she stands tall and in a saree she is a reason for lust. She even has light eyes. Mine merely brim over every now and then.

I want to see my father and then I want to meet that moneylender. One of them is a thief. One of them has taken away from me what my mother has. I have been dealt a poor hand. Beauty, the playful beast, has skipped a generation. But why should I be so drab? Why should I look so ordinary?

I was harsh with my mother as daughters are but more so because she was so good-looking. I could have done so much more with what she had. In time she passed away. When she left me I needed adoption.

I have seen the priest, the temple savant. I do not tail him but I do go to where he stands bare-chested, where he sings to the gods and rings a bell and I see him eyeing the worshippers closely. I have no strong feelings towards him. Other than hate.

My name is Sandhya. I am a spirited girl. People don't know me. I have my mother's disposition and like her I can be mean to myself.

* * *

SANDHYAKAAL

And then I got married. I got hitched. I was drawn up close to a male of the species. Not for the first time, mind you. This nephew of a friend of my mother is and was a fine man. He was not a go-getter, nor a climber of the company ladder but a man who could knot ends that would never meet because he loved to buy better, live better and spend. He was a dreamer too, a man who wanted to be a writer. He did write and I read some of what he had penned. Nothing much to say. I mean he had nothing much to say, really.

We started our conjugal innings in my mother's house that was in between Rainbow Colony and Cenotaph Road and while it was traditionally built to begin with it went under the knife so to speak under my husband's guidance and emerged looking like a plastic job. If you walked past in a hurry, you would have missed it. It was typical and it was nondescript. Like my husband.

The house had a facade and a name. Illam. All around me straight lines met and formed right angles. The architect was a builder. And the builder was a mason. The mason came cheap and he took orders. The one place that was still mine was our garden. It looked like me; untended, verdant, weedy, wild and a green lush with a few surprises.

All the rooms in our edifice were rectangles except the living room which was a square. Doors happened where lintels formed and windows sprung up here and there. In one lucky place a tree looked in.

Amidst this ode to plainness the flooring stood out. It was white, polished mosaic. It was laid in situ by Madurai Meenakshi. It was a cool expanse that invited bare feet. The doors were made of teakwood and were well polished. The teak tree must have been old and frail because its wood aged badly. The whorls cracked. I could see faces in them. I could see middle age.

We have four wheels now. After a decade of scooters we have a sedan. It is parked on the road. I can see its upraised backside. I can hear it clatter when it starts. The scooter is now parked inside under a cloth cover. One day I will learn to ride it. My husband promised to teach me once this happened and that happened.

We stay alone.

I watch soaps every evening. Soaps give me a family life. I am the daughter-in-law. I am always newly married. I live four lives every half an hour, every day. I have four husbands vying for my attention. There is one who has mine. I got married on the promise of a soap every evening; a daily unfolding of episodes that would hold my life together.

* * *

Words occur to me. One such word is endowment. My husband speaks of it. I believe it is a financial term used by insurance companies. It is a fund into which you deposit driblets every month and this is a private hundi that steadily grows into a decent sum that you encash at the end of a period they call tenor. Unless your husband dies before his tenor. Then you get the sum assured. Sum assured? Yes that is another term. You give thousands and the sum assured is lakhs. You give lakhs and it is crores. Dizzy. The sad thing is if the insured person lives you make less money.

Guptaji is an uncle I was asked to meet. He is an astrologer who reads palms, faces, charts and such. He is an interesting mix of homespun advice, humour and occasional gravity. I am a manglik, a dosha that is devastating for marriages. My husband knows and fervently believes that pooja and gemstones can staunch the red planet Mars.

'Show me my lifeline,' I ask Guptaji. 'Is there a sum assured?'

He laughs. He is a wicked fellow.

'I have seen your husband's hand,' he tells me. 'He has a lambi umar but with many jhatkas.'

'Illness?'

He doesn't tell.

'Money problems?'

'Ah, Laxmi,' says Guptaji. He spreads his hands, conveying helplessness. 'She is the most fickle Goddess.'

'Guptaji, tell me something I don't know.'

'You are a Manglik and your husband is a karma chameleon,' says Guptaji. 'As per his horoscope and yours, he should be dead by now.'

* * *

The bell rings and a young fellow enters. He is wearing a smart tie. He sits at the edge of the sofa and subtly looks around at my house. I offer coffee which his training manual has told him to accept. It gives him time to get comfortable. Finally he pulls out some brochures and makes his pitch to my husband.

He speaks of 'The Great Indian Accrual'; a method of investment where inches precipitate in your jungle. He waxes eloquent about 'diversification', a portfolio approach where birds of all species shed feathers and live in utter harmony. This young fellow poisoned my husband's mind. He made him deposit driblets in 'The Great Indian Annuity', a harmless LIC Policy that would pop when my bubble burst.

I am distracted by all this money talk. In my mind are a million mutinies and a lifetime of going against the grain. I let him have his say and then ask the crucial question.

'What is your minimum portfolio size?'

My husband looks surprised at my question. The young advisor hems and haws. I know my husband is a writer and needs no wealth management.

'Do you offer loans as well?' I ask pointedly. I get an angry stare from you know who.

Ten minutes later I see him off. His parting shot is, 'We also help you transition.' He sees my raised eyebrow. 'We help you plan your estate; stuff like making out your will, rationalizing your assets before you pass on and so on.'

After he is gone I sit for a while and think. I should be doing what he says. I hate enumeration but I ask myself, 'What will I leave behind?' This becomes a gripping question, a metaphysical hunt. After I am gone what remains?

That night I dreamt of a world without me. I had truly expired. I roamed where I once lived. There was no road in my name and no mention of my life in school textbooks. On my anniversary date nothing happened.

I woke up in a sweat and searched for something, anything. I found him, my hand at his hip and he thought it was the urge and he took over, clambered all over half-asleep. When all was done, bar the shouting, I lay back and looked up at the ceiling and thought about endowment. I wanted an endowment fund for males; a well-endowed fund. I was willing to pay to see something grow from small to big. Get me an endowment scheme, show me the form, fill it up.

'How was it for you, my dear?' I asked the mirror in the morning. A tender enquiry. There is no such thing as a small mercy.

* * *

Illam is a fuck house that stands on a fuck street with no fucking setback. Windows are closed most of the time. That way I do not have to dust twice a day.

Today is a bad day.

I am on the ground floor, a plinth that is two steps above the earth. It is here I wait for the rains to abate. When it rains like this the water rises and waits at our doorstep and then wets my feet. And I am standing and merely watching. Something has happened. I have no idea what.

An hour later I have to move the furniture. I find things I thought were lost. I find my marriage certificate behind a chest of drawers. That piece of paper is more than ten years old, signed when I still had a flourish.

I climb to the first floor. There are eleven steps. The fourth is broken and the seventh is chipped. When you go up you stumble, when you come down you trip. There is one light in the stairway in the small landing. Insects collect here every evening for a meeting and wings break free and fly away.

I climb to the second floor. It has a terrace. The terrace has a water tank, two satellite dishes, a parapet wall and fucking redemption. The flooring is rough and uneven.

Sitting by yourself every evening, waiting; that is the bleak moment. Waiting for the night to advance so you can sleep; that is the dark moment. Giving up at 4 a.m. after a fitful night; that is the dawn. Routine arrives at 6 a.m. The clock strikes me down. I have anxiety for breakfast. The clock melts at noon. It creeps up on me in the evening. I have shadows for dinner.

My husband eats Manekchand gutka for breakfast. One packet goes down after every hour. The packet has coated crumbs. It has hard betel that has wedged in his teeth. The fragrance hangs around him. I have married Manekchand. I read one day that Manekchand bought a Maybach. I deserve a fucking ride.

Marriage has given me many small moments. He does nothing dramatic. He is not a despondent fellow and is generally cheerful. I have never seen him sad or worried. Nothing befalls him. He works in an office. He commutes in a car. He lives in a home. He has a wife. He thinks like an auditor, so he ticks boxes. There is a check-box for children we cannot have.

I shut the doors at night. He locks them.

Say something. Tell me something. Does somebody up there have a grand plan? Is there some magnificent schema? Or am I here on this earth merely to come and go? I read epics. I watch the giant classics. I now believe these things never happened.

NUMBER 24

GUPTAJI'S PYJAMAS ARE CRISP and his thoughts are slowly moulting. He is ensconced on the single-seater sofa with his hands wrapped around a cup of tea, a Green Label brew with two drops of milk. The pot sits on a side-table, its snout looking askance. He speaks in his measured manner, weighing every noun and holding the reins on these verbs that in 'modern' times have turned frisky. He often lapses into the past tense treating it as a friend and ally. And the future? Well that was strictly business. 'The pre-ordained nature of our lives' sums up his worldview.

In the past few weeks he has been dropping in incessantly 'to lighten the mood'. He has been pushing Sandhya to adopt a child.

'It is there in your janampatri,' he told her. 'There is a boy,' he said. 'His name is Vedant.'

I would adopt a girl, Guptaji, a girl called Aradhana.

'Get real,' replied Sandhya. 'And get married,' she told him.

Two weeks ago on a festival day Guptaji had come with her horoscope and had spread it out on the table to do a new reading. She had looked over his shoulder and inspected the planets seriously. 'Where are my ovaries?' she asked him.

Her voice gave way as she said it. It wasn't much but I spotted it and so did Gupta and we looked at each other and at her. That inflection was a cry, a vulnerable moment, a thing of beauty when a person you know to be strong realizes that something she wants so much is not humanly possible because someone somewhere has dealt her a hand, or charted this course whilst she wasn't looking. Is it possible that a person needs to break down to recoup herself? I think so. In her case it will never happen.

Every sip of tea causes Guptaji to consider the previous and the deepening brew reaches the tipping point when the cup is lowered and the pot is pushed away.

'Every marriage has an overarching theme,' he said. He said it in Hindi and his voice had softened. 'For most people it is children. You don't have any. So what is yours?'

Surely the house?

The plot belonged to Sandhya as did the modest structure that her mother had built. She entrusted the rebuilding to me. This was to be my moment. I razed the existing structure and built a new one. It took eighteen months. There was room enough for the two of us and none for children. It lacked an overarching theme. And perhaps inspiration.

* * *

I went through a phase when I saw myself as a Sufi. I thought Baul singers were Sufis. Some painters like Swaminathan and Bawa looked like Sufis. Nusrat sang like one and so did

Kailash Kher. Writers like Rumi wrote in a Sufi shorthand. What was it? Was it about looking rustic, dressing folksy, smoking a beedi and having a reedy voice? Was it embracing the abstract and singing songs to an unnamed Universal Being? It is hard to describe that one quality these Sufis surely possessed. When it was there, it was visible as the plain light of day and yet it was a fleeting glimpse that eluded capture.

I built the house during this phase. A spare structure and a simple construction, it was devoid of trappings and had no superficial elements. It turned out different. Did it have to look like a dull blob?

'This house is the death of imagination,' said Sandhya. 'I cannot get the right words to describe it. Not that I care.'

'Try aesthetic.'

She doesn't think too hard. Her careless view hurt more than anything else. Those were the days when she had ceased to care about a number of things, about how she looked, about what people said and while all this spoke of a decline in our relationship she was past listening.

'Look at it. Here, come outside.'

I refused to be dragged.

'Don't just sit there like you are on Death Row.'

I walked out reluctantly. But I looked at the neighbourhood.

'Look at the others on the street,' I replied.

Right next door was a Telugu house that gave itself away with its showy misplacements: an ornate balcony, a floral insignia in gold, a daring chhajja and a sudden swooping roof, each competing with the other. Inside I could imagine a sweeping staircase and mirrors in strange places. Two houses away was the house of the Gulf returnee. It beggared description. It had no elusive quality other than taste. There were many Brahmin houses in this Co-operative Colony and they were recognizably austere. The walls were cream, the windows were a military green, a corridor led from the front to the back and a stairway that began near the entrance swivelled and turned to the verandah on the first floor where the next generation cooked eggs, drank Kalyani Black Label and did other no-no's like listen to 'Tragedy' while smoking Charms. And then there was new money at the T-junction where a traditional house underwent a fancy upgrade. New money fluttered and preened and in the hands of a young architect it showed up as glass bay windows, wood cladding and chrome detailing amongst the staid brickwork. The surplus funds went to work and evoked a trellis below and festooned a pergola above.

Amongst these Number 24 was mute; a silent spectator to its own anonymity. It had concealed wiring and plumbing and no salient features. This lack was a conceit it seems; it was deceitful to build a house and give nothing away.

You could have done so much better, Kumar, berated Sandhya. Even a clichéd, parochial place would have worked. A house that said, 'Staying put here in this structure is Mr Kumar, baniya of species, sitting on palang, one leg folded and one leg up, chewing rupaiya and spitting image of his forefather who roamed the street with foodstuffs and tilak on his head and one hand in the till, prying and also trying it seems to flee far from his forebears who tilled land, ate the meagre crop and forgot to pay the moneylenders.' It was quite a speech.

Apna Ghar we say in Uttar Pradesh. Ghar jo bas gaya hai? Never. No. 24 was a place that never settled. I have a scar on my face to prove it. My floor has lard, fat, makkhan, churn from a pot, stuff that grows in udders, a milky way that takes away your sure step and makes a mockery of your time on earth. Lard is the food for ghar jamais. Think of me as an interloper in this place. A ghar jamai? Yes, called a veettu mapillai locally. There is no better way to say it for the connotation is cultural and the ignominy of staying in a place owned by your wife is best conveyed with an Indian tongue. Kumar, the ghar jamai is a loose appendage that hangs by a petticoat thread, a kachcha dhaaga. This thought buggers me often and it lurks in everything that Sandhya says, in her every look and her implied tone. I am a lesser man somehow on my two feet. I should have walked away.

'I know what Sufi is,' says Sandhya. After one too many she knows most things, like the colour of burgundy wine and amber whisky, the taste of caramel rum and the honest notes from each that she sniffs at and describes as if she was a connoisseur.

'Ask me,' she says.

'Am I one?'

She shakes her head from side to side with a hint of regret, happy to say no. She feels what she wears with her fingers, a gossamer something made from sheer muslin, cut with imperfection and gathered loosely at the waist. She twirls a strand of hair absently, reminding me of the early days when that very gesture made me melt. In my mind I am a culpable man for the things I have done to her which she has never felt.

'You are not cut from the cloth that makes Sufis.'

I am not. I am hindered by the stop-start nature, the punctuation in my life, in my stories and in my business enterprise. This morning I woke up thinking about Death. Death was an early bird that was foraging in my garden. My fear was that swaddled in my blanket and waking up I looked like a worm struggling in the sand. So did others, I hoped. And then I survived and this thread led nowhere.

Ranga is like me in this matter. He is another victim to the sporadic nature of some lives. The two of us are fooled by the promise of a linear progression. Yet we do what we do, karmanya vaadhika rastu, two donkeys standing outside the Vivekananda College of Learning, weighed down by the bojh of a dhobi, two asses who have eaten strewn pages of a Bhagwad Gita and have been so condemned to unquestioned labour without fruit. Maa faleshu kadachana.

Ranga's house was built in instalments. Like his life it resembled a ride in an unreserved compartment in a passenger train that shuddered to a halt whenever a station showed up. I saw it come up as I stood at my window. The scenario kept changing and comfort seemed futile. Money came to Ranga in driblets and he added to his house whenever he could. I knew how he paid for it. Inbound groups paid good money and so he could erect his structure. Outbound tours had misers or, more truthfully, normal Indian families who drove hard bargains. This paid for his furniture. The bric-a-brac that filled his home was cheap stuff bought from handicraft sales from Madhya Pradesh, Rajasthan and Gujarat. These were guilty buys made at closing time on the last day. I accompanied him and tut-tutted as we heard the craftsmen relate similar tales of woe.

At night Ranga's abode was lit up and it showed the decline of the Indian sensibility. It started well in the living room with Post-Colonial, a time when Corbusier was busy and furniture was elegant and made from real wood. You came into his bedroom and it was low-lit using uplighters and a suspended globe made of craft paper from Pondicherry; here is when the Emergency was declared, a time of national disgrace when Ranga ran and hid in his college for he heard that they were pilfering souls and cutting cocks. When that storm blew over he went to the bathroom and let it all hang out. Liberalization took hold here and imported soaps like Camay and Lux unwrapped themselves and shampoos mingled with conditioners and they sat next to an unused toilet roll because the arse-wipe was a visibly filthy habit. The only place that resisted the march of history was the bar. The bar was a bottle. When the bottle diminished another took its place. The makers' name was Solan. This was their No. 1 whisky.

Ms Sandhya is the house owner of No. 24. She has the patta. Her fingerprint can be found on the document in the Registrar Office. Her right thumb is there fresh from the inkpad, pressed down by the Assistant, leaving a telltale mark of her genealogy. I saw it take shape, this circus, this medley of actions that bestows land. We returned to a place we could call our own. A few weeks earlier her mother had passed away. She appeared one last time in *The Hindu*. She was wearing spectacles and looking at me as I read her remembrance. I felt guilty. It was a jumbled-up time. Sandhya was a mess because she felt cheated. The good Lord taketh, she said. He came a tad early. And without appointment.

'If death is a common cheat,' says Sandhya, 'then life is a betrayal, no less. This life should have taken better care of her time.'

I have to blurt out something at this point.

'Your mother…'

'Don't,' she warns. 'Don't say anything about her.'

'Fine, women then.'

'What about women?'

'Women are of two types. One lot who go through life looking for a culprit. The other who stand around like Pieta.'

'Which one is my mother?'

'There is a third type,' I reply weakly, beating the retreat. 'That is your mother.'

And then I lie inert and pretend to be dead. And finally when I cannot be moved she tells me what she thinks about me.

'You know, writers have so much to say. You are not like them. You are too quiet, you imagine yourself to be some sort of a mystic and so you keep your silence looking to others as a wise and all-knowing intellectual. It doesn't fool me.'

'I am proud of my silence,' I blurt.

'Bah,' she replies. 'See.'

See what?

'Nothing is making sense, so I am quiet.'

This isn't a schoolboy escape. This is my everyman answer when presented with a woman too complex for my means.

* * *

So many years and the full bloom was past us. We were not hungry anymore and what remained was disquiet. The house was central as a theme but staying in it we had a new companion. It wasn't Guptaji, though he did come by often.

'The overarching theme in our marriage is not the house anymore,' I told him.

He drank his tea with some gravity.

'The house is merely a catalyst.'

He raised an eyebrow.

'It is silence, Guptaji. What do I do with that?'

He understood exactly what I was saying having sat long enough in our midst.

'Write about it,' he said.

* * *

I walked behind a woman today. She wore a perfume. It was a dated fragrance. I could imagine the small, precious bottle of Eau de Cologne placed on a dressing table that had an oval mirror. Made in Paris. One dab behind each ear and a drop on the left wrist. A perfume called Intimate. I followed her till she crossed the road.

The wind had changed direction. This came from the land and headed towards the ocean. The morning breeze was warm and gusty. It didn't feel right.

On my return there was rain. It was a sharp, single shower. I stood under a tree for a while. A schoolteacher stood by me. 'How are we today?' she asked. I wagged my tail.

At home it was the usual quiet. I liked that. I wore a board that day that said 'Don't talk to me'. Sandhya locked herself into her room. I heard the clink of ice on glass. That would be 6 p.m.

I tried to imagine silence. There are so many ways.

I remembered an obscure tomb in Delhi that was heralded by a misspelt sign. I found a buried Minister. He was a functionary who had made an honest mistake. He was hung with honour and they gave him this space for all the salt he ate. The grounds were overrun by wild bushes and the tomb had a tree growing out of its dome. When I entered, the leaves rustled. And then nothing. I sat there for a couple of hours like a solitary reaper. I left when two lovers came by.

Those were festival days and the maidans of Delhi were festooned with tales of Ram and Raavan. There was a mela in a wide open space and in the middle there was a merry-go-round. It was afternoon and in the bright sun there was hardly anybody. The machinery was turning and there must have been a tune but I could not hear it. A single girl rode a pink horse and they went up and down and around. The man who was turning the wheel was lazy. It was a slow ride. Something made the girl's head turn. And what she saw made me freeze. A Raavan on stilts walked by noiselessly, his many masks looking.

And then the rain, always the summer rain accompanied by its precursor, the loo, a dry and dusty swirl that brought clouds and lightning. I walked in the rain up to Ring Road. Water had collected near a drain. An old woman took the ends of her saree and dipped it into the swirl. She squeezed out the water, flapped the cloth and wiped her face. Our eyes met. She said nothing.

* * *

I returned to Chennai by train. A journey that I cannot remember. I caught a bus at the station.

The only conductor in Chennai is in a bus. He balances precariously with a bag on his shoulder, wads of tickets of various denominations are lined inside it and he holds a metal punch that clicks audibly and it is this sound that stays with you. The bus is riven in half with the left side for ladies and the right side for the studs. In the middle are limbs, hair, jasmine flowers and chappals. Between one bus stop and another is a single movement with its allegro and its concerto. Every gear shift can be heard and every brake stomp can be felt. As you stand during the journey you read the poetry of Thiruvalluvar etched above the windscreen. It is written in Tamizh of years past and makes no sense. In the warm humid weather you shift from one foot to the other and get intimate with a stranger. You alight at journey's end at the depot.

The depot was silent. I walked home. I sat in the verandah with Sandhya for a couple of hours. We did not speak. She asked me nothing about the days I was away.

Silence is not the same every place or time. The silence of the dear departed is final; the silence of the living dead is inchoate. In No. 24 it is the silence of reproach, of disquiet, of a seething enmity of purpose. It is one where wavelengths never meet.

I didn't choose it but this is my silence. This is my keepsake, my erstwhile haven and now my nemesis. Around my modest abode there is noise of people living. A Govardhan plays his flute. A woman derides her company. And a street dog yelps at the newfound piss on his tree. And there is me writing a book that speaks louder than my engagement with a woman who for some fucking reason keeps her silence. Like I do. We are both worthies in this Gumbaz where even whispers would echo if we ever let go.

'Pranaam, Guptaji.'

He pauses before he leaves.

'Kumar.' His hand is on my shoulder. He wants to say something, the only thing that will break this impasse.

'Nothing,' he says finally.

* * *

'Sandhya,' I call out loudly, breaking the silence.

She doesn't respond. I check her room. She isn't in. She must be upstairs on the terrace.

* * *

On the terrace a pair of jeans flapped because the breeze was stiff.

A towel tore loose, flew off the terrace and fell below in a heap.

Mankind walked past in shapes and sizes.

Dogs buried themselves in sand.

A street vendor called out to every window that had a curtain.

And I pulled the plug.

Nothing very dramatic, mind you. I left home with a small bag of essentials, two bottles of beer and enough gas in my car to reach the Marina beach. I finished my beer, got out of my car, flagged an autorickshaw, and caught a train. You do this without thinking and that is why you do it. Reason is the thief who robs you of purpose. Imagine going to Central Station in the night, standing in line, buying a waitlisted ticket and catching a train to a place you never meant to go. I did it. The Nilgiri Express departed from Platform Number 4 at 9 p.m.

The ticket collector was an accommodating sort. He found room for everybody, especially stragglers like me.

'Name?' he asked as he prepared a challan.

'Sandhya,' I replied. And then I used my maiden name. 'Sandhya Ramdas.'

HALF TICKET

'I DON'T KNOW MY AGE.'

This reply is not in the Railway Manual. So what does he do?

'Where are you from?' He asks rudely.

'The place has no seasons. It has mango trees.'

The ticket collector is stumped. He looks helpless. He should be going for there are empty seats that have takers and there are bribes to collect. But this half ticket holds his attention.

'Who bought you this ticket?' He looks at the printout suspiciously.

'My father. He is a miser. He said a half ticket would do for me.'

The compartment looks on with bated breath. The fan rattles, the wheels click and a man in the upper berth snores. Is this insolence?

'You look honest,' says the TC finally. 'But your replies are vague. And you have a faint moustache.'

He looks towards the other passengers for support. There is an old woman travelling alone, a young couple who move apart under his gaze, and on the side berth a lady with very little luggage. They smile in different ways. He punches the ticket and hands it back to the boy. The hand that reaches out has a ring on the middle finger and the palm has cuts that have healed.

'Next time ask your father to buy a full ticket. Moustaches do not deserve half tickets.'

The boy says nothing. He has a rucksack on his back that he hasn't taken off. He is sweating profusely and looks ready to jump up and run.

'I am letting you go,' says the TC. 'But my colleagues will not,' he warns.

The boy looks at the counterfoil and then at him. He thrusts his printout towards the TC.

'My name is there,' he says. 'The spelling is correct.'

There is a quiet titter from the passengers. The TC is speechless. What do you do when a boy who looks so earnest speaks to you with a straight face and yet his replies could be mocking you? He snorts and clicks his way down the compartment.

Nobody speaks for a while. Lights are switched off and beds get made. The boy looks out of the window. He is seated still. He speaks aloud to no one in particular.

'I have no brothers and no sisters. My father has grey hair and my mother died when the rains came.'

The old lady clucks sympathetically.

'I have never been to school. My friends have all left for the city.'

'Are you also going to the city?' asks the young girl. Her companion shushes her.

The boy shakes his head.

'I don't know my age. Nobody knows. In my village there is no new year,' says the boy. 'We don't keep calendars. We don't need one. There are no holidays in the fields.'

'Diwali?' asks the girl. 'Birthday?'

The boy looks at the ring on his hand. He runs his fingers over it. It has a pale blue gemstone.

'I was born on full moon day. My father said I will be trouble all my life.'

The lady on the side berth introduces herself to the others and gets chatting.

'My name is Sandhya,' she says.

She keeps an eye on the boy and finds him intriguing. They reach a station. A few vendors come to the window and offer tea, packets of food and magazines. They are all turned away by indifference.

'Chhokra,' shouts one of them. 'Take this package.'

As the train leaves the station the food packet stays in the boy's hands. He looks at it and places it on the side table. The packet leaks from the side and the liquid runs off and a puddle forms on the floor.

'We grow rice in my village,' says the boy. 'We do not count the grain.'

The young man wants to end this monologue. It is late and time to turn in. His girlfriend has climbed up and is looking at him meaningfully.

'Stop pretending,' he tells the boy. 'You are not as innocent as you seem. Everybody knows their age.'

'Mataji,' says the boy. He turns towards the old lady. 'What is your age?'

She laughs and reveals gaps in her teeth. Her hair has thinned and her skin has wrinkled, but her eyes are young.

'Beta, I do not know,' she replies. 'Now it doesn't matter. Better to not know as you grow older.'

The train has gathered speed and the rhythmic sound and movement should induce sleep. But something is unresolved amongst them. The boy should remove his rucksack but he doesn't. He should remove the food packet and stop the leak but he doesn't. He should introduce himself and explain himself but he does not do so.

The young man with the girlfriend is irritated for some reason. His life is in good order, every year has been held to account. School, college, job; every milestone has been met through diligence and hard work. He is now plotting his marriage and his posting. This young farmhand of unknown age is cheating and play-acting and getting under his skin.

'What is in your rucksack that is so precious? Why don't you take it off and go to sleep?' he blurts.

The boy cries softly. His head falls and tears run down his cheeks. This changes things. He has people on his side now. They watch him silently. After a while he removes his rucksack and places it under the lower berth. And he walks out of the cabin. He doesn't return. And nobody in that compartment could sleep thereafter. In these trying times a show of emotion and a piece of unattended luggage can ruin your peace of mind. Somebody needs to do something. After what seems an hour the TC returns. He peeps in and finds prying eyes.

'I offloaded the fellow,' he says triumphantly. 'He didn't

want to get off and he started crying again. I told him for a half ticket you get off half way. I had to push him out.'

The old lady looks horrified. 'Where would the poor boy go in a strange place?'

The TC shrugs. 'He was not a boy. Did you see his moustache?'

'What was his name?' asks the young girl. She needs that part of the puzzle.

'His luggage is still here,' says the young man. He points below the berth.

The TC scratches his head. He had forgotten the fellow's rucksack. Now he feels bad. He hauls it up and checks to see if it is locked. It isn't. He opens the straps and flips the cloth cover back. And he removes the contents one by one.

There is a book. 'Shaheed Bhagat Singh,' reads the TC. 'Biography. In English.'

The young man snorts. 'I told you he was a fraud.'

Next to come out is an item he has foresworn knowledge of. It is a calendar with a God photo. 'Shiva,' says the TC, 'With his consort Parvati.'

'The fellow was carrying a calendar, the cheat,' shouts the young man.

'Today's date has been encircled in red,' says the TC.

The last item that comes out is a ticking clock.

'Wait a minute,' says the TC. Attached to it are some wires that lead to a battery pack and what looks like a lump of clay. He looks at the time and he sees the second hand approach destiny.

'Mar gaye,' says the TC.

LEAVING HOME

WHY DO I FEEL LIKE I HAVE LEFT HOME? There is an aching finality, a sensation of loss. I need to touch the cold floor, place my hand on a latch and open a familiar door. I sit up god knows where. The floor at my feet feels fine and the latch on the door is mine. I look up. The ceiling is shut with my rafters and the fan with three blades has a familiar whir.

The window lurches into view. The view is mine.

Breakfast will help, hot tea will help and the morning smoke should clear the cobwebs.

Kala the maid is on leave.

Drag those feet to the kitchen. Ash trails behind.

'Oodbatti,' says my dead grandmother into my inner ear. I hold the cigarette between my thumb and forefinger. I hand it to her.

'Theepatti,' she says. I pull out a matchbox and light her up.

I called her Paati.

'Pohai,' says Paati as she breathes in the smoke. She saw me light up my first in my teens and never ratted.

I saw her go up in smoke. The smoke made faces at me and I must have said something for people looked startled and realized I was a girl at the ghat. They lead me away in a hurry. I walked backwards till I could see no more.

The water boils as I hunt for leaves. It is still on the boil as I light up a cigarette and stare at the backyard. There is a crude bird's nest perched on a water pipe. It looks ready to disintegrate. A feather breaks loose and descends, swaying with no purpose.

I remember now. I had dreamt of flying the coop.

My room is untouched.

I am coming home again.

Most mornings I used to awake with this thought of returning home.

Deep into the night I was the silent wanderer. I dreamt of fleeing. I was the banished king. I was the seeking Gautama. I was the roving minstrel.

Nobody asked for me.

Two sadhus greeted me on a deserted road; one called Dharti, one called Dhara. We smoked in silence.

I returned to my famished kingdom and ate a banana.

'Sambrani,' says my grandmother, my beloved Paati.

She is bowed as she walks each room, holding a chalice with fragrant smoke. The smell creeps into my clothes and makes me cough.

'Sambrani, kanna,' she repeats with affection. 'Good for you.'

Her forehead is bare. Her white saree is in disarray. I

watch her spine and count her vertebrae. If she straightened she would break.

That chalice sits on a mantelpiece, unused since she left. Every time I get close it parts with a whiff.

It is a day like any other. I can never remember a thing I did in the morning. Perhaps it was all routine, perhaps it wasn't. There was silence. I spent my days spelling words.

The afternoon was the worst time. I used to fall asleep. There was a nodding sensation that lurked at 2 p.m. It waited for the meal to be ingested. Stupor was so colourless.

Sitting around and doing nothing I have had blank-outs. I have emerged an hour or so later and paid a bill. The waiter has spoken and it is a reply. The meal I have eaten has a leftover.

I am not home right now. How is that possible?

'Karpooram,' says the grandma finally. She places an irregular lump of camphor on a large spoon that has a black discolouration. Her hands shake as she strikes the matches. One of them catches and she drops it. She invokes her maternal side loudly and curses the paternal. I help her out. She watches me circle the flame. She slaps her cheeks and pounds her ears with her fists. She almost topples over. I perform the aarti.

'Drop it on the ground, Sandhya; don't stamp it, you little devil.'

I watch warily as the flame dies out. My feet are denied. She cackles at my disappointment.

I needed new windows. The position of the sun and the opening in the almirah met. The clothes were fading and the mosquito gauze had dried wings. If I had shifted each window, I would have had a new room. I would have aged differently and my face wouldn't have had wrinkles where it lay.

I have moved windows before but the ledges stay. I can never let go of the ledges. There is one in the house which I cannot get to any longer. There is one which became a shelf. It is there that my authors gather. They rewrite. In the morning I pick up crumpled pages.

At night I hear them speak.

'One day you will be like me, Sandhya,' says my wrinkled grandmother.

I look at her closely. I look for room to manoeuvre, room to improve. My grandmother was feisty but she was a feisty wreck. And she smoked on the sly in the small toilet in the outhouse.

'I will be better than you,' I shout.

She sobers at the thought of me growing old. She looks at me anew.

'Never be a widow,' she says. And she looks here and there and drops her voice. 'If you are smart, you will manage it.'

I took her advice.

I have an audacious garden. A water body has formed on its own in the centre, as if by right. It is the place in the sand where the water from the roofs descends during the rains. In it is a wilting lily that refuses to die. There are four crotons; stout fellows with knobbly knees and twisted leaves. They wear ugly well. A riotous bougainvillea has taken hold near the gate and it is scaring the daylight. It has formed boughs, it has stitched curtains and it has embraced a parapet wall. The flowers are fighting with the leaves and winning. I have a bird-bath under a tree and birds drop seeds and seeds take hold and plants sprout roots and stake their claim. I stand amongst weeds and feel like a well-groomed guest in my garden.

Can I be buried here in my own garden? Who should I ask? I have never understood why people do not choose to bury themselves in their patches. Every time I have visited an obscure tomb I have felt jealous. They are insanely beautiful. I am talking of these small tombs that people say have gone to seed. Nobody visits them. The masonry has chipped, plants are growing in the walls and on the dome, creepers have wrapped themselves around the gate and the courtyard is sprouting weeds amongst broken bricks. I find the setting irresistible.

They have not gone to seed. These places are home to people.

Every time I visit a cemetery I feel sorry. They are so well maintained and have fresh flowers, yet I feel sorry for those below, clubbed as they are with strangers. I wouldn't want to mingle with strangers in the after-life. Don't believe me? Dig them up, any one of them. Tell me about their grimace and their pain.

I stay on a road called Cenotaph Road. I cannot think of a better address after I am gone.

I lost a dog a month ago. He wasn't just a dog. He was my companion. I cannot bear to use his name. He saw me as he went and his eyes spoke to me clearly.

Dogs have more expressive eyes than humans. Domesticated dogs have a challenge; they have to communicate every day with humans. We are dumb in their measure so they make up in ours. They develop different barks, they invent new postures and most of all they look at us in different ways. I tried talking to my fellow initially and there was no response. I realized that talking was about tone and had to be accompanied by gesture. My friends said, 'How well you have trained him.' I laughed. That was mere performance. The fellow makes me dance. He has games to play and the personality of a card sharp.

My dog looked at me as he went away. I got the message. I buried him in my garden. Nobody knows. There is space enough next to him.

* * *

The party is in the evening and it needs a pooper. I have tasted everything on the sly. There is too much zest in the iced tea and the wine is on the boil because the chiller is in a sulk. Too much is going wrong with the salad despite a dressing down with flakes. There are olives in two colours and cheese in three. I tasted them. Neither of them can taste salt; there is just too much of it. Oh and there is a bake as well that isn't rising.

'The kitchen suffers most when you are not around,' says my grandmother. She is sunning the annuals and the seasonals in the terrace; vadams, karvadams, pickles and spices.

'I know what broke your back, Paati,' I tell her.

She straightens a wee bit and then expels breath. It comes out with a rattle. She looks surprised at the sound. She holds my shoulder.

'I think it is time, kanna,' she whispers.

Later that evening she asks, 'Will you adorn me with flowers when I am gone?'

I ask no more of my garden.

The garden looks green after the rains. What a sight greets my undeserving widower. He has done nothing in the time he has had. He has planted nothing. Today he has hired help to clear the place. The fellow he has called is a manicure artist. That bastard will make a clearing in my jungle. He will trample my weeds. The widower wants to present his friends a fresh new space devoid of all I left behind.

I do not have much time.

The first time he broke my stride was when we got married. He arrived at our first meeting looking askew. His clothing was dot perfect; Indian traditional, crisp and visibly new. His mind was elsewhere and I resented that. Nobody comes to meet me as a distraction that they have been led into.

'We'll see to that,' I said to myself.

Within a couple of hours he lost his diffidence and misplaced his spectacles. He fumbled and spilled the salad. The dog came to clean up, brushed his leg and he dropped the plate. It was ceramic and it shattered. The sound brought a smile to my face and he saw me smiling. That unguarded moment gave me away. The next one hour he got after me. He tried to get under my skin through questions and mild taunts. I let him. As we stepped out into the garden he broke my stride. It was deliberate. I got into a tangle and I remember being really upset.

How did he know? How in the world did he know that the one thing that put me off was this? People on two-wheelers and drivers in cars have learnt that they cannot break my stride. I am used to tyres screeching around me. I am used to the smell of burning brake linings. If I am walking as I am every morning down Rainbow Colony, nobody can break my stride. The right of way is mine, granted by decree.

So this sullen guest who came like he had been dragged, decided to change his mind and get my attention. He got in my way. The pointed heel of my right foot landed where his toes must have been. He was wearing Kolhapuris that were a pale brown. I felt flesh and bone. The commotion took half an hour to subside. The bleed took longer.

We got married and he broke my stride again. As we goose-stepped around the holy fire he stopped suddenly after three circles. I was barefoot. No harm done. We bumped into each other and the end of my glorious red and gold dress flirted with the flame and caught fire.

He was grinning, unaware. 'She is in a hurry,' he said loudly.

I chased him like Hanuman in Lanka. By the time they caught me the flame was sizable. I still have that designer dress. Every year some flakes drop off.

We broke up but we did not part. Our house was a cementing force that we could not resist. It was large enough to give space for us to ruminate. The routine in the evening was always a flashpoint that needed to be negotiated. There were two entrances to the house and three exits. The additional exit was at the rear and it led to a side street. The side street was a leafy lane. It had a single street lamp at the very end. On dark evenings it would be quiet and empty. Every time I left home at that time I felt cameras shooting the scene. I would walk conscious of hidden eyes. My car was a small cubbyhole on four wheels. It had a belter of a music system and a benign engine. I would coast the streets and music would set my pace. I was an irrational driver and following me could be frustrating. On blue days I would meander and rock n' roll would have me thumping the side of the car. Cars that followed me would overtake, the windows would slide down and the drivers would shake their fists animatedly and say a few words. I would mouth a response that begged to be printed.

I would drive around with a face pack. I would have my hair in curlers. I would be wearing slippers. Once I wore kajal that spilled and spread. A policeman saw me at a traffic light. You should have seen his face.

Driving around the city was a two-hour routine. I would return satiated. On my return there was nobody to ask where I had been. That saved me a difficult answer.

The third decade came upon us and the game had changed. Too much had happened with each of us that we were unaware of. Marriage had acquired a new syllabus. There was no need to take stock. Just call for a meeting every month. Be civil. Some embers have died, brother.

We had an arrangement. I am not telling too much here. I rolled my own cigarettes. I used the leaf it came with and I mixed it with happy-go-lucky. I smoked in the dark. Every time I smoked I had an affair with a gentleman. He smelt of tobacco and reeked of shadows.

Take my advice. Take a drag of angel dust and sip some water. Every time you inhale you accept your body. The exhale spirals out of my nostrils. Just one for the day, remember.

What a downer.

He hasn't sold the car. It stands parked; six month's dust has collected below it. The seat length is mine, the rear-view mirror meets my eye and the gear lever is on second as I left it. What is he waiting for?

What am I waiting for? I am busy populating the pages of a diary. The thought that I can people some sheets is exciting. For me verbs are exciting. Verbs like ghost-writing have a freshness. Verbs like party-pooping have potential.

Somebody is knocking on wood. It is a repetitive sound.

It is him. It is a habit that I found irritating. He is at it again. He is nervous about the evening because for the first time he is hosting it without me.

I am raiding the bar like I used to. He has locked the cabinet like he used to.

Take the forceps and use it like a lever. Open the cabinet and grab some ice. Drop it in a glass to hear that sound. Roll the glass around. Hear some more. Get the amber liquid. It comes in a golden bottle. Hold it against the light. Always see the colour. Today is good, the light is mute, the voltage must be low. Pour without a measure. Once the ice floats you are fine. Leave it on the ledge, the ledge you have left behind. Tighten the scarf around you. Fold your arms around yourself. Wipe that little speck of lipstick that smears your mouth. Your ring will sparkle. You will catch yourself in a mirror. The sight of you never changing; you can never change. Once a cube of ice slips, raise a toast. The first sip should not be delicate. You have to feel some fire descend your throat.

Luck is on your side, brother. You have had another day without incident. This evening you will find familiar friends holding glasses. You will count your blessings, knock on wood and raise a toast to your wife who left you. And tomorrow you will look behind every door and below every chair for signs that my shadow lurks.

Dear Diary

It is my birthday. You just told me.

Dear Diary tells me all. It has confessions to make.

The party is in the evening. The party needs a pooper. I am the one.

The fucker is planning a remembrance for me on my birthday.

People should know he is faking it.

Some days things go wrong. He needs to know why.

'Kanna,' calls out Paati. 'Look what you have done.'

IV

THE FUNCTION

I THINK IT WAS THE FIRST DAY of a month I cannot remember. Or perhaps the last day of September. The day I rescued a moth. At a time when clothes were drying, at a time when women were sleeping. At the hour when clocks strike one. At the very moment the tap ran dry. It rained.

The streets needed a wash.

'The weather is changing,' says Chithi, my 'blood' sister. She is gathering folds to tuck into her midriff.

I snort into page seven.

'The weather guide shows a round circle with three lines.'

She smiles as she ties her hair into a bun. She pokes a pencil into it and does a twist.

'Athimber is coming,' she adds.

I snort again. 'He is always coming.'

Athimber, her sister's husband, is a bank employee. He works for a Nationalized Bank. That makes him a species of leisure.

'He wants to become an acti... something. Actually an anarci... something.'

I look up from my paper. Activism and anarchy did not go with Athimber.

'Serious?'

She adjusts her saree, pulls the pallu behind her and looks at herself sideways.

'He told me he got a bill for one and a half lakhs from the telephone department. The next day his electricity meter reading showed nil usage for two months and the electricity fellow wrote 'tampered' on his card and went away. And finally he got hauled up for jumping a traffic light when he says the light was not working. So how could he jump it? The policeman said 100 rupees with a wink or 500 with a challan.'

This is interesting. 'So what has he done?'

She places a red bindi on her forehead and gets it wrong. It is too high. She frowns and that makes it right.

'He went on vacation for a month.'

This is delicious. 'And when he returned?'

She places the nozzle of the cologne below her arm and it hisses. Notes of lime and lavender pass by. I sneeze like dogs do.

'He has started spluttering. He was always very emotional. I remember he cried once when he visited a hospital.'

This Athimber was that Athimber; the one who sprayed spit when he spoke. He was a nervous sort who had gaps between his teeth that came from chewing his nails.

'I am perishable, I say,' he sprays. 'I have a shelf-life like upma.'

He suffered from maladies of the mind. His principal fear

was being rendered redundant because his job at the bank was low-tech. He handled telegrams. Telegrams went out of fashion along with trunk calls and his skills needed reset. He moved to telex. He worried when telexes' tenuous hold was challenged. Then the facsimile came and he watched and learnt. When email happened he came up to me.

'What is phishing?' he sprayed. 'Somebody is always asking for the bank's password.'

* * *

'Is it still raining?' I ask Chithi.

She looks towards the window.

'Drizzling.'

'Who else is coming?'

'Mapilai is coming.'

Her husband and my brother-in law is a cussed fellow in family matters. This is a surprise. He is called Mapilai by everybody, just as Chithi is called Chithi by all and sundry. In my wife's family, incest was common and uncles were often younger than you and aunts were also your cousins. This family had no tree. It had a maze of cross wiring.

'Mapilai wanted to know if he should bring something.'

* * *

I walk in the light drizzle and take in the smells. The street dogs look wet and ragged. They shake themselves vigorously and then shiver. There is one furious specimen that I like. He has a harelip and a leer. I call him Biscuit.

I drop in at the Xerox and Binding Centre. A young boy sits at a desktop with his head in his hands. He looks up as I enter.

'Not ready, sir,' he says. 'Your punctuation is very bad. I revised colons and semi-colons. I removed apostrophes and I redid the conversations.'

'You whatdid my conversations?' I blurt.

The boy was getting too smart.

'Did you like the stories?' I ask. His feedback was important. He was the only one who read word for word.

He nods a little too vigorously. And then he asks, 'Sir, will I be in one of them? I have never been in a story.'

'Yes, of course. That is why I come here.'

He looks at me like a puppy dog and I realize just then that I know nothing about him. I take out a notepad and pen from my pocket.

'What is your name?'

'Varadarajan, sir. With 5 A's. My father's name was Ananthanarayanan; he had 7 A's.'

'What do you do, Varada, besides this part-time work?'

He enumerates and picks one from his list.

'Sir, I am an artist.'

I ask him to come home after he finished work the next day.

* * *

Chithi and I go shopping for puja samaan. We go down Eldams Road. As the road nears Mount Road the temple comes up on the left and outside it are the roadside shops with all the requirements for any puja. How do you choose a shopkeeper? My Chithi has a regular. He holds a rope that dangles from the roof and he bends dangerously over piles of malas, coconuts, camphor, agarbatti and bananas.

'What puja is it?' asks Chithi. She is irritated at the lack of focus in the buying. I am taking two of each.

'Two coconuts? One for puja and one for chutney?'

She tosses her hair.

On the way back I look at her profile. She is aware. She has to say something.

'I never knew you liked ritual. You were such a hothead in these matters.'

I look out of the autorickshaw at the angry skies.

'Do not ask too many questions.'

She has always been there for me. Amazing, I just had to call and she would come.

'Chithi, I...'

'Don't say it.'

* * *

'Cameras make you smile,' says my niece.

She holds the point and shoot away from her as she takes a picture. That is the modern way; no need to squint into an eyehole. I find her fingers small when she wraps them around anything. She is small.

I smile.

'Can you erase that please?'

I do.

'No expression, Uncle. Nothing.'

She half depresses a button and I hear a discreet whir.

'No, don't go blank, Uncle. I need a face.'

I attempt a state of limbo. I think character. I talk from the corner of my mouth.

'Will you cover it for me tomorrow evening? It will not be long.'

'Two Archies comics,' she says.

I was thinking Amar Chitra Katha. I give in.

'Uncle,' she says and pauses.

I await the denouement.

'Will you cry?'

I probably will.

* * *

Sleep is a state of knowing nothing. You awake and search. That is the first thing you do. You need a point of reference to anchor yourself. Mine are a pair of spectacles and a watch.

Time of day: a.m.

Position of self: repose.

Light: semi-darkness. Sandhyakaal?

Today is the day. It hits me. I spot the one thing that sets me on my feet. A photograph of me and her; the beach behind, blue sky above, the wind in her hair, dark glasses perched on her forehead and a halter dress that threatened to slip.

I take an ache and put it away. I file it for later. The mind is a whir of things to do.

* * *

Time: p.m.

My niece will be there with a camera but there will be no cake.

My Chithi will be there with the puja samaan but there will be no deity.

My Athimber will be there full of questions.

Mapilai will come with a customary bottle but there will be no glasses.

The boy from the Xerox Centre will come to say his piece.

Two uncles and two aunts will be there in their traditional finery.

My wife will be there in spirit.

I have done it again. I have assembled the family for no reason. I think they indulge me.

I am alone among the atrocities. Bloodshot. There is a curfew on ghosts. I am reading Agha Shahid Ali aloud as I used to when she was around on some evenings; evenings of despair when she was lonely enough to seek my company.

The harsh light of the next morning peeps through the sunshade. I gather some thoughts, lean on an armrest and write. The night before was spent in the company of the missing.

I spend the day writing a story. For her. In it I age and I become a Mittal. Sandhya is a singer, a talented one. And we live in another time.

I hope she reads this story and stops hounding the space near the bar cabinet every evening. A man needs a drink and his solitude.

V

THE STORY

KAUSALYA SUPRABHATHAM

ACCORDING TO RAGPICKERS' LORE the old man and his dog were found on Marina Beach every morning, facing the water as if they were looking for somebody. No one went up close to them. No one heard what the old man was humming under his breath. It was a mellifluous rendition of something. It wasn't a familiar Suprabhatham.

* * *

'Some days in Chennai you cannot buy a cloud,' says the cop.

'Pay for it,' says the chaiwallah, stirring the large vessel on his thela with an oversized spoon. The tea boils and gurgles when he stops.

The cop slurps the dregs from the glass tumbler and spits some tea leaves to the side, grinning at the thought of paying, allowing it to amuse him. He will not pay. This chai shop is unlicensed and at his mercy. They both know it.

'One day you will pay,' says the chaiwallah, half in jest and half inured to the injustice meted out by this mamool.

The cop spits to the other side. He is a seasoned vyapaari. His boss was an adhyapak in the art of squeezing value from the street vendors. They never had to buy vegetables. And this chaiwallah was a North Indian, a Bihari, a migrant like many others who were flooding Chennai. They had no standing with the constabulary.

The old man walks past them with the tethered dog, a small black and white mongrel that has the build and restlessness of a Jack Russell. One eye has a black patch and the other is pure white. His ears fold like origami and perk up in different directions. He is a lithe beauty if you like that kind of thing.

'Biscuit,' says the cop gruffly. He rests his weight against a tree.

The chaiwallah opens a glass jar and parts with a coconut macaroon. It is crisp at the edges and spongy at the centre. It is also slightly stale. The cop sniffs and takes a small bite. He makes a face and throws the rest towards Jack Russell who wolfs it down quickly, his eyes and ears darting looks towards them. The cop loosens his belt, opens the top button on his khaki shirt and fans his insides.

'Brahmin,' he mumbles, looking at the old man, hating him. He burps a falsetto.

Nothing has value on days like this. Idle sunshine. Inertia. Heartburn. Passersby dawdle at the stall. Cigarettes sell. Nobody has manners.

The old man receives their attention. They note his polished forehead and envy his fair skin that is stretched tight. Three vertical lines mark him as a devout Shaivite.

He has a gaunt frame, grey hair and an air of uncertainty akin to an unresolved theorem. He walks without lifting his feet and the dog trails behind him sniffing at sand piles. When they reach the main road they wait patiently for the traffic to abate. Waves of two-, three- and four-wheelers pass by. They cross in the company of a helpful cyclist. It takes them a few steps to reach the outskirts of Mylapore where some houses have washed their entrance, a few scooters have left for work and a singular tamarind tree has dropped its pulpy fruit. The old man picks a few and chooses one. The tamarind is finger-licking good. It is measured on a register called 'pulippu' when raw. Ripened, it mixes a sweet tinge with the sour taste. Either way his teeth will hurt.

The old woman is there as usual. This is his Kausalya. She has bathed. Cold water has washed her skin and kept her young. She wears a worn silk Kanjeevaram with a thin brocade border. She has been to the temple already and parted with a one-rupee coin in remembrance of someone long gone. She remembered the face but wasn't sure the date was right.

The two glance at each other. It is a casual glance. The old man wishes one day to stop by her gate and part with his discovery. He has a scientific temper. He had made some important discoveries. He could predict the flight path of the house fly. He had married saplings and developed a fragrant bougainvillea. And he had found a new musical register and a superior Suprabhatham, a breathtaking morning entreaty that he hummed in his head every morning at the beach hoping to bring the extra-terrestrial to life. He had to share it with Kausalya.

A crow flies by with its misfeasance, flapping its warm breath in his face. Not today. The day did not feel right. He walks away.

A body that has weakened but a head that has stayed still despite the advancing years. A mind that he put to the test. On his surreptitious visit to Vidya Mandir, his old school, he had peeked into his senior classroom and spent a few minutes in front of the blackboard. Two chalks and a duster were placed on the teacher's table. He took a chalk piece and wrote in capitals on top of the board. A thought for the day.

BLACKBOARD SITTING IN THE DEAD OF NIGHT.

He could go mad thinking of the minds that had walked this way, these benches of hard wood where the young had spent hours that passed slowly, and that light, that window and that form, those thoughts of escaping.

'We have travelled,' he whispers. 'This is my music.'

But his mind wanders. 'This, my land has been encroached.'

It was true that unsavoury elements had come to Mylapore, the last bastion, the lonely agraharam, to the place where his ancestors formed a club and organized kutcheris.

'My great-grand and my grandfathers and grandmothers sat in the Mylapore Club amongst karma yogis and when they walked in Luz Corner the earth did not own them. Theirs was a Brahmin mantra. Who could sing it?'

Only those that had Sanskrit in their armoury and mandalas in their brains. The old man doubles over as a sharp pain strikes his midriff. He straightens as it subsides. He mutters under his breath.

'Forlorn are my days. Sick are the nights when age catches up.'

On a good day he has a cough, a limp, a hurt shadow and a dread of the unknown, the one unknown that drives him to distraction.

'Brahman,' he shouts. Brahman is the only forebear he will acknowledge. The other elders are dead and gone. 'Bring me death so I know it. Let me decide when. Why should the last move be played by another?'

And so said, he slipped into his own skin, took his breath into his two canisters and walked his dog away.

* * *

He remembered his running battle with a college teacher called Gnyanam, a word that meant knowledge and a man who belied his name. Gnyanam hounded him in every class from first year to the third. He was a Christian convert, in his eyes a lesser being for having opted for a New Life or a paid Christian brotherhood. Gnyanam must have been a quota recruit in this Christian institution. How else could one explain his lack of English skills, his poor temper and his insecurity? He wasn't fit for purpose but he was feisty. Every look he found offensive and every class conversation was directed at him. The back-benchers were out to get him, he felt.

'Are you a Tamizh, Brahmana?' asked Gnyanam, as he stood before him after his nth misdemeanour. They were alone at this hour in this stray corridor that lead to the staff room.

'Who is asking?' is what he wanted to say. But he stuck to a less insolent, 'How do you say yes, Sir?'

He meant it. The language of yes he had seen. It was a true riddle just like Gnyanam. Yes is a Brahmin term he felt. Why can't the Brahmin understand that no is the territory that breeds what it takes?

The teacher is unsure but he laughs all the same. They stand for a while each contemplating the other, one looking for hidden meaning and the other biding his time. The insolent student makes his move by inserting his hand into his shirt, bringing out the sacred thread and raising it to his eyes.

'What have you lost, Brahmana?' asked Gnyanam, gloating in all that the Brahmins were now denied, in the recent triumph of the lower classes through activism and political endeavour.

'I have lost respect,' he told his teacher, making no secret of whom he had lost respect for.

Gnyanam slapped him across the face, once. And let him go. No one was around to see this. Punishment was so simple and one-sided. He hated it. He yearned for complexity. Emotions like a celebratory rage. Or in Gnyanam's case a fulfilling suicide.

'Sir, you are a failure,' he told Gnyanam. He was walking away and out of range.

* * *

The Brahmin has a manifest. Not a manifesto. A rule book. Not a statement of exceptions. It is true. Brahmins in South India believe in facts that are backed up by numbers. Grammar gets respect. There is little room for opinion.

Brahmin boys will do well in a choir. A Brahmin girl will excel if allowed to. Stick her with dance classes and she will do tha thai thaka thai. Parade her in front of relatives and she will sing 'Kural Undrum Illai' by the book. Samathu penn. Do the samail, braid the hair, tie the knot. Freshen up every evening like it matters. Don't ask for a pension.

It was a time for exceptions.

Kausalya is a trained classical singer who learnt from the age of seven. Her talent was discovered by a Telugu Vidwan who overheard her singing near a stream at a height of 6000 feet in Kodaikanal. The family had gone for a holiday to this hill station and in the morning cold her brothers were brushing their chattering teeth while she was trying to stay warm by singing aloud. Two phrases and the Vidwan felt a breeze where there was none. It seems she sounded like the doyen D.K. Pattammal.

Kausalya was also a Brahmin like the doyen, but unlike the latter her family was keen that she performed. She was diligent with her riyaaz, singing along with the greats and then when no one was listening she would branch out on her own, taking with her a private space that she filled with song. In a matter of five years the major ragas were in her grasp. She had no interest in performing. Efforts at organizing a family gathering where she would be called upon to sing failed. She was like a mule in these matters.

Why are you learning then?

Stupid question, she retorted, tossing her hair. And she broke out spontaneously into a Kalyani of such power and grace that they forgave her. She had the pipes. And she had an emotional connect to her audience. She sang like she was asking for something. (Her life, maybe?) Her mother cried. Such a sad rendering, she said. What's with this girl of mine? What sorrow she carries within her? Is this a rebirth?

This girl Kausalya will go far, said the relatives, pointing into the stratosphere where evolved Brahmins were watching. It was rare for someone so young to be so involved with her music that it showed.

'When she sang at home the trees grew,' said her Maama, a closet poet. 'Nature listens to its ilk. Can't you see she is a force?'

Nobody understood what he said.

'Kausalya, come here,' called the elders.

They wanted her to touch their feet and so be blessed.

'Marumagale,' whispered others, each a prospective father-in-law.

And why not? A daughter-in-law of this calibre was hard to find. She was short but her hair was a long kundal. She had everyday looks but she was fair. She ticked most of the check boxes, looking occasionally demure and carrying herself with grace. Little was known of what took place behind the make-up and beneath the bodice. There was a fire for sure and it wasn't meant for the kitchen.

It was assumed that her marriage would be to a successful person who would nurture her talent and allow her to flower. She had no such ideas.

'Poo?'

She disliked flowers. The one time in the year she sang in public was in December in the environs of a temple. This temple was a modest one but it had an enclosure made of rough and unpolished granite. It was open to the sky and one end of it was adorned with some unfinished stone carving that looked quite abstract. It was a strange place but she liked it and here she would give it her all, starting low and slow and building a single raga for an hour whilst listeners sat enthralled. It was a thing of beauty. It took place at 8 p.m. By 9 it was done. Elders would not rise for a few minutes after she was done. Should they incur her wrath by asking for another? They should have. She would have lasted the night. The girl that said no all the time was asking to be wooed.

One youngster, a boy who looked a serious type and who sat in the front row and finished a surreptitiously brought-in packet of bajjis, understood what was going on.

'I know what she is trying to say,' he blurted.

'Makku,' said his uncle, cuffing him behind the ear. 'Dolt,' he added. 'Do you even know what comes after Sa Re Ga Ma?'

The young boy looked pained. 'Maama, it is a call for help,' he said weakly.

He had seen it in her eyes. He had seen her confusion. The girl wasn't sure what she should do with her life.

'She is that type, Maama.'

'What type?'

'A type,' mumbled the lad.

He had seen these people. His maths teacher, a brilliant failure was one such. Hopeless types who did nothing with their talent and had a prodigious nature because it came too easy. They felt superior compared to the sweating hordes who inched ahead of them every day.

He went up to her, shifted from one foot to the other. He ended up merely looking at her from close quarters, trying to pry further secrets. This girl was a treasure trove of strange feelings. Being next to her he felt different. They had to drag him away. The girl noticed him. He was sure of that. Why else would she have tossed her hair in his direction?

For two days and three nights he composed a

conversation. It veered towards poetry, of the kind his Maama wrote and tore up for fear of being discovered.

'Should I learn music?' he asked himself finally.

And he did. As was his training he learnt the metre not the song. He learnt to recognize ragas. He learnt to fault people for slipping up, for going astray, for trying and not succeeding. He became a music critic.

Later, much later, he did meet her once. Again standing next to her he divined much of what she was all about. His Maama would not listen to him, so who could he tell? This girl was afraid. He knew.

* * *

She had read the classics. She had seen with dismay the fate of Draupadi and Sita and Meera. She had dutifully sung Sita Kalyana Vaibhogame, a song that spoke ostensibly of Sita's wedding but ended up describing only Rama. From the second line that said Rama kalyana vaibhogame the song extolled the groom.

Son of Lord Vayu. Beautiful of bearing. Nourisher of devotees. Bestower of enjoyment. Terror of demons. Peerless body and unique hero.

Stanza after stanza poured praise on this Rama.

Garva manava, said the song; beyond the ken of men of arrogance.

Can men go beyond that? Did Rama? No, said the women. She agreed.

She had sung bhajans to Krishna, mouthing the words as a child and later discovering their meaning. She sang many of the Meera bhajans that M.S. Subbulakshmi had rendered so beautifully that it hurt.

'Daasi Meera prabhu... Morey to Giridhar Gopal doosra na koi.'

No, sir, not for me. No ghungroos for me. She hated unrequited love and a life in its service. Meera was beyond her understanding.

As for Draupadi, she thought the Pandava was not a worthy prince.

What hope was there in family, in marriage and in love if this was the position of the male pantheon?

* * *

As a young man he did ask himself, 'Am I worthy of her?'

Should he have gone to her house and confronted her with: 'I know what I will become. I will be a middle-class breadwinner earning a modest sambalam in West Mambalam; a meagre salary that will fight inflation, which will provide enough to subsist within a moral code. That we will be careful goes without saying. It will be a good journey (a second-class coach, a lower berth) if you can keep the end in view. But you will not be restrained by me in any way, or asked to do what you do not wish to.'

He should have.

Kausalya knew he existed, knew what he wrestled with. She needed him to come up and say his piece on that very night when she had sung in the temple, her grand moment so to speak and this lad had stood in her vicinity trying to summon up courage. She would have told him what he needed to hear, 'When they meet, moments of weakness surpass the great.'

* * *

She married a North Indian, a Mittal, a connoisseur of the arts, a man who could distinguish a Yaman from a Kalyani.

'He does not bother me,' she said. 'He does not attend my concerts. He stays at home. He looks at news channels and remarks: "Desh ki chaddi gayab".'

The sights and smells of the other life were strangely attractive. The Hindi kaaran was fair game. He came from the North evoking a rashtra bhasha and an allergy. Mittal came from a large family of six kin and two miscarriages. He was the other, business-minded to a fault and forever out to make a profit.

'Our houses were kept apart by euphemisms, not a boundary wall. It was a small colony. What could you hide? We shared without intending to; festivals, food smells, nocturnal creatures, feathered friends and a watchman called Periaswamy, an old fellow who had a daily battle with a cough and a maid. Holi and Raksha Bandhan were shared festivals. Diwali was a dovetail, a day earlier for me.'

'Mittal, oil your hair,' I would say, the night before. On those days he wore a traditional dhoti which was white and he would pull up the ends between his legs looking quite rustic. He would wear a white cap as well and a flaring red tika. He had a moustache flecked with grey that drooped downwards.

'Mittal, you look like a farmer approaching a nationalized bank for a crop loan.'

He would smile, ever so slowly.

'I am from the cow belt,' he would reply.

Mittal was never in a hurry and seemed to have resolved a few things in his mind and reduced the rest to insignificance. He was intelligent. I liked his eyes, the slow gaze that took in everything. He seldom spoke out of turn.

His bond with music came from another world. It is as hard to explain as perfect pitch. Before him the others paled, their applause sounded hurried. Thehraav. He had it. With an audience of one I could rise. I needed to. Subtle is our language, our respect and our need to out.

We never made love. It wasn't in the equation. There were young men in the vicinity. He sent one to me on a pretext. What he did not want is a sub-plot behind his back.

Sex is a divine rhythm. Isn't it? Taal. Miley. Nadi. The depth charge of a mridangam, the sharp rap of a tabla, the base of a pakhawaj all paled before the charming rusticity and gathering peak of dholak and daphli. This wasn't my music, but who cares. The body listens. I will live. Death can wait.

* * *

She affixes a bindi, dead centre, an open well, eyebrows are tributaries, with a single bend, trailing into a single strand that looks to be in some danger of curling upwards. Kajal, black, darker than black, waiting for eyes. Red where the hair parts, a signal red, alert, a marker, a construct. Breath, enough to fulfil space, what rises falls, no drama here. Love.

Love?

Laughter.

Read my lips.

Can't.

Never look at the lips of a singer. We are contortionists.

She sang through the night. An alaap that evoked the divine, a taal that followed the rhythm of her hand beating her thigh and finally a tired threat of a love song. The morning came, amenable to a bribe. That was then a day of silence, of assent. When she was resigned she was welcoming. Come to me, the forbidden for the singer, anything cold, anything sweet. In the evening she was lost and could not be recovered. This was a vulnerability that could take her life. Did chance keep her alive? It was faith.

Faith, given enough room to evolve, nurture and breed a less callous nature. Faith is a mother, the believer a child, held sometimes to ransom by times that call to question belief in a movable cycle of chance.

The one clean space was inside her head where she dwelt, a distillate of soul and a republic of ideas with just enough room for doubt. She really wasn't sure that all she carried would stay and all she married would stand. But she cared.

'I have grown to like him. I took a chance. What is so precious? He saw me through puberty, keeping an eye, till I sang just for him one day. It was a Hindustani raga. Darbari. Halfway through, his eyes watered and he made no attempt to stem the tears. I still don't know why but it was precious.'

'What did you see in him?'

'Imagine him as a sounding board.'

'Precious?'

'And precarious.'

'You were together till...'

'He passed on. He left on a Saturday like he promised.'

'Promised?'

'You won't understand.'

'Try.'

'Saturday was performance day. He said he would leave with my Bhairavi. He was ailing for a while. He wanted to die at night. It had to be Bhairavi or Malkauns. I would have preferred the latter.'

'Hmmm.'

'Understand he did nothing useful in his life. Nothing. He came and he went. Like many others.'

'You never despaired?'

'Sometimes. Initially. Then I said for whom? He seemed fine. When he died I stood next to him, rooted, running myself ragged, my stomach a pit hole and tomorrow a threat. He was too old for this and I was too young. He did say this before he left.'

'Take my tomorrows, run with them.'

'And do what?'

'I don't know, make something cruel?'

'Like?'

'Like age. He was right about age. I have asked this question before. If age has been given a number, why does it need a sign?'

'You mean like the colours of your autumn? Or the sag of your muscle?'

'Age is just one day. It will come to you for just one instant. One day I will not be able. It will come. To hear myself sing.'

* * *

With the passing days (they did pass quicker every year) he had earned the sobriquet 'old man' merely by ageing. He was now a senior person. This entitled him to a few things. He got a seat in the bus even if it meant someone getting up. He received offers for help in crossing the road. And occasionally he could jump a queue. What he never understood was why such courtesy came in the way of his thinking.

The last twelve years were solitary. He could roam of his free will. His time was his own and there was no set routine. There wasn't anybody making demands. And yet in his House of God a large black Nandi bull blocked the entrance, its rump a solid mass and its small tail a curious size. Only dancers knew the way past.

He had applied thought using first principles. All the years mastering mathematics, physics and chemistry came of use. His building blocks were sound. And yet his perception ran into a wall every time he tried to cheat the pale of death and look beyond.

What lies beyond this life?

A simple question that surely deserved more time from his scientific brethren? Instead, they wished to explore matter and its avatars in the Moon and Mars. They were sitting next to radios listening, waiting for signals from other places. Damn you buggers. He was frustrated beyond reason. The final frontier was not space but the life beyond each of us. In his reckoning there had to be a simple switch, hidden, waiting to be found.

This fruitless quest of his begged one final question. Are we incapable of knowing that the way to this understanding is barred?

He asked Kausalya. One day he picked up courage in his sleep. He phrased his question a little too eloquently.

'Why can't I be privy to what happens when I die?'

She smiled. His heart warmed. And she set him at peace.

'Treasure this lack of knowledge,' she told him. 'It is a tender irony. Either that or it could be the last betrayal.'

He remembered trying hard to understand what she had said. And watching him struggle she simplified.

'Don't expect the Post Office to address your concerns,' she said.

* * *

'Who is this old man?' asks the chaiwallah. 'Must be a retired government servant or a teacher with a pension that met his needs as long as he kept them in rein.'

'He is the music critic for *The Hindu*,' replies the cop. 'I know where he stays in Mylapore. Musicians of all types come to his house and touch his feet.'

The chaiwallah laughs. 'They touch his feet? Of this old fellow? You have seen it?'

'Yes.'

The cop knows more, a whole lot more. He is an inquisitive fellow. He is paid to be.

'He is in love with this old woman who stays a few doors away. She stays alone in a helter-shelter place where stray dogs lie, cats get fed and crows gather in the evening because she leaves something for them as well.'

'Anything for food,' says the chaiwallah. 'Creatures are so smart.'

'You are an idiot,' says the cop, with some feeling. Migrant fellow. 'That woman is a classical singer. In the evenings she sings. That is why the creatures come.'

'Nice story,' says the chaiwallah, looking at his vicinity. He has dogs and cats around him too and crows in the branches eyeing his leftovers as well. All he did was play the radio now and then.

'Yes,' says the cop. 'A love story.'

He spits some tea leaves, this time into the breeze and scores an own goal.

VI

THE RUNT

RAMANATHAN

He sat in the same place every day. He was a man of letters.

He had an independent air.

He told his son, 'I will stay with you. I agree to that.'

He built another floor.

He built a staircase that took off next to the gate. It lead to a verandah on the first floor. The verandah had a low ledge, a low-slung chair and a small fan.

* * *

His skin was like parchment.

His teeth were on edge. His molars had ground and his incisors had lost their sharpness.

He ate rice that was boiled till the grain clung to each other. The wife then mashed the gruel to a paste. This was meant to aid digestion. The stomach craved for more.

He sat in the same place every day. He wore white.

He was well read.

* * *

He reads.

What the well-read man is wearing is a line
Cut from cloth that makes dusty jackets.
When he sits, hardbound books crease
around his middle.
His spine is a binding that has eyeholes and threads.
When he talks, you hear the voices in his head.

* * *

He writes.

LETTER TO THE EDITOR

Dear Sir,

The thing is I have become tired. I am a man of infinite patience. But it is trying to sit and watch what is happening. I have no grievance against people making money. I myself have made some: enough to enjoy the evening of my life.

But some of the people who are making money have no moral code. They are oblivious of what is right and what is wrong. Should I allow this to happen? Can I use my advancing age as an excuse?

The wife interrupts. She shouts as if he is hard of hearing.

'Iyer, go get the milk. The van has come, did you not hear it?'

The milk van is a full-sized truck. It is custom built with

row upon row of blue plastic carrels which have neatly stacked white packets of milk. There is a queue. A line of maidservants mingles with male help leading to all kinds of chatter. Iyer Sir is allowed to get ahead.

The place smells. It is difficult to describe the smell. Every day the truck parks in the same place; at the T of the junction. It drips some oil and that spot is black. It also leaves behind a puddle of milk where the carrels are stacked.

He buys. One litre for coffee and one litre for curd; all his life it was one plus one. Before the truck it was a man on a cycle with a cow by his side. The cow had a calf by its side. This threesome would come and make conversation. The chap has moved to the suburbs it seems.

Iyer accosts a child who is playing with a stick.

'Have you seen a cow?'

The young boy shakes his head and looks at him wordlessly.

'Have you smelt norai, milk foam?'

The boy nods.

'My chithappa has buffaloes,' he replies. 'They are black and they can swim in mud.'

Iyer is disappointed. He has one more question that the boy surely could not answer. But the brat speaks first.

'Thatha, if I eat grass will I give milk?'

Iyer has thoughts in his head as he reaches home.

The wife is standing at the gate and staring. Her hair is loose.

'What happened to you?' he asks her loudly. 'You are looking like Bhadrakali.'

She is clutching the gate as she stands. She is slender, he notes. In a couple of years she will be frail. She points. Her gnarled finger is bent but it points in the right direction. It points to a new restaurant that has opened opposite.

'Iyer, do you have eyesight?' she asks.

Iyer blinks a few times till autofocus kicks in.

* * *

That evening he sat in the verandah without a newspaper. *The Hindu* lay inside, crisp and unsullied. The folds had not been tested. In front of him was a blank sheet and the fountain pen was unopened. There was a letter in his head but he did not feel like writing it.

The next morning he goes for a walk without glancing at that board. He reaches the park near D'Monte Colony and sits on his customary bench. His group senses his distraction. They walk in circles. He remains after they have left. His head is bowed, his fingers are animate. They are typing words. Occasionally he pauses; occasionally he recollects. He remembers the names of the cows he had and the calves that were born. He flinches when he recalls the size of the injections that the vet carried. It was violence the way the cure was delivered, the way life was injected. He used to hold their ears while it happened. He used to stroke the skin folds that hung from their necks and calm their doe eyes.

That night he tosses and turns. He flits between his childhood memories of a dairy farm near Myladithorai where he would be busy from morning till night milking cows, preparing their feed, watching them graze, piling the dung and washing their sheds. They would sell milk but give the curd for free. He remembered calves being born; the initial terror turned to joy as the black calf took its first steps.

He woke up late.

'Iyer, the van has come.'

Later that morning he sneaks a look as he heads out for his walk. The board is painted red and has black lettering.

SANDY'S CAFÉ

Below the name is the death knell.

STEAKHOUSE

Iyer writes to editors and to activists. Most of all he writes to appease his mind. This place has to shut. How can they? The Co-operative colony is a Brahmin creation. This is not meant to be a place for beef steaks and madu curry.

'Why are you looking so constipated?' shouts the wife. 'Should I give you your mixture?'

Iyer grunts and his abdomen winces.

'I am not in the mood for your mixtures.'

He is tired of gruel. He is tired of man-made paste.

He scowls at the milk van. He scowls at the packet that is dripping. He scowls at the smell. He looks at the line of people waiting. They look like meat eaters.

After three days he writes a sentence.

If we separate the cow from the milk we will get people who eat beef.

That night he tosses coins as he sleeps. Heads and tails crowd his mind. And offal litters his bed.

* * *

LETTER TO THE EDITOR

Dear Sir,

I write this as I sit at my desk.

A carpenter made this desk from wood.

I saw him make it.

I wish I had seen the tree. If I had seen it, I would have stopped him.

Yours sincerely,
Iyer

RAINBOW

IT ALL STARTED WHEN A STRANGE PHENOMENON showed up on Google maps. An aerial view of a small road in Chennai showed a well defined rainbow. It wasn't an animation. The news of this phenomenon spread and people called people to know if this was some kind of virus.

The thing is it rained at that very place at that very moment. There was a cloudburst in that obscure street in Chennai. The residents welcomed the arrival of the monsoon by running onto the road. Why would they? They could not see the rainbow. It was night time.

Junior liked the thought of a rainbow at night. He liked the thought of beauty that is unseen, much like music that is unheard or epiphany that isn't felt. These things did not belong to anybody. They existed but you couldn't own them. Like people's lives.

The place is called Rainbow Colony. Rainbow Colony has just thirty houses that are ranged around a single street.

The street is barely 300 yards in length and is narrow besides. The development can be called intimate. The space is like a crucible. Daily routines intersect and lives criss-cross.

The Colony was peopled by middle class Brahmins who had joined a Government Corporation and retired from it. The job was steady and their progress was a slow inch perfect. Salaries rose in tiered slabs and promotions were predictable. In all these long years their gaze never wavered. On retirement they discovered their pace of life hadn't changed.

What do they do now? They echo sentiment. They speak in one voice when they rally behind their leader Subbu. Subbu was a ring leader in their office. He was their current spokesperson.

'I can talk,' he said succinctly. 'For everybody,' he added.

He was famous for the sudden pause.

'Every pause,' he says. 'Has an effect.'

The colony was by and large a peaceful place. People who stayed there valued placidity and treasured boredom. They preferred to read news, not make it. Most of the house-owners had two children each of whom had done their engineering or medicine and had flown the coop; with the exception of Ramanathan. Ramanathan had just one son but enough trouble. The boy wore his hair long and played the guitar. In his room he had posters of Freddie Mercury. The rock star was in tight leather pants and without a shirt.

'Grow up, you rascal,' Ramanathan kept shouting. 'All you do is sit at home and eat sundal.'

'I want to write,' announced his son.

Junior was a budding writer. He had a fountain pen and a thought every day. He had a pen name too.

'Show me what you have written,' said his father.

The boy refused. His writing was complicated.

The boy was gay and was discovering himself.

'Stop passing gas so loudly,' complained his father. 'Stop eating sundal. Go do some physical work.'

Junior had finished college some time ago and had done well as per the mark sheets. His heart wasn't in job finding, office working and life living. His father's sedate lifestyle depressed him.

'But he is such a bright boy,' exclaimed everybody.

'He is a tubelight,' retorted Ram. 'He flickers.'

'Let him study if he wants to.'

'He wants to study some more so he can sit in the campus and polish his bad habits while I pay his bills.'

Junior was polishing his writing. While his friends studied in college he would sit inside the vacant cricket stadium in Wallajah Road in an obscure stand and write.

'It could be dawn or it could be dusk.
The light is the same.
But the birds give it away.
The tired day is winding down.
I thought the world was waking up.'

Most of what he wrote got rejected.

* * *

Junior had just rejected the nth wedding proposal. When pressed hard he could not come up with a reason.

'What is wrong with her? Look at her, she is beautiful, she is intelligent and she is my cousin's daughter.'

Junior wasn't looking. He had already found love. A Nepali boy who was a drummer on the loose. He had smooth skin and lustrous eyes. Junior wanted to spend the rest of his life with him. He wanted to bring him home and keep him. But what to do? His father was a diabetic and a heart patient. His nerves stood out like swollen, green streams near his temples. One of them would burst for sure.

The matter was urgent but kept pending.

Another pending matter was water supply. The previous year had seen very little rain and the lakes had run dry and so had the sumps. Water supply was by tanker lorries and each load was getting more expensive. The members of Rainbow Colony got together and called a water diviner. A chap called Arumugam showed up. He was wearing a dirty veshti, his hair was matted and his breath smelt of alcohol. He had a permanent leer. Arumugam went into each house with his magic wand looking every inch a sorcerer's apprentice. The women hid behind curtains and watched. The men hid the valuables.

After a couple of hours of trawling the neighbourhood the idiot stood in the middle of the road and quivered. Arumugam was loath to leave the centre of the road. Beneath him he felt a turgid stream. He was sent away.

The Colony met again at Ramanathan's house. Everybody trooped in and found some seating. Mrs Ramanathan served her famous sundal but held back the drinking water.

'Arumugam says we have water,' announced Subbu. The rest perked up. 'But it is deep underground.'

That was deflating. The bad news was they had to dig deep for water. Arumugam had warned them that the water source felt fickle and would not flow if the dry spell continued. He had suggested 200 feet deep to be on the safe side. That meant additional costs.

A proposal to dig shared bore-wells was discussed.

'Those whose houses are used for the shared wells will have to be compensated,' said Mrs Narayanan. A few nodded. They understood why she had raised the point. She had the best 'oothu' according to the water diviner Arumugam. 'Very strong flow, Madam,' he had said. She had leant over him while he had gone to ground in her garden. Arumugam's wand had fluttered in her presence.

'Madam,' he said breathing deeply. 'If I dig a hole in your garden your water will break at 20 feet.'

Her proposal to charge money had an objection from Srihari, her immediate neighbour, who argued that no money was due to her since the rain water drained into her ground from his plot as well. He had a large plot and it sloped towards her house.

It was a stand-off. Srihari went ahead and hired some labour and dug an open well near the boundary to Mrs Narayanan's house. Mounds of earth and clay piled up on the sides as the hunt for water began. Water oozed in and the well filled up. Srihari waited till levels rose and he installed an electric pump. And he stood over the gushing water in full view and read the morning newspaper while the rest hand-pumped.

'Copious flow,' he remarked to Mrs Narayanan. He caught her peeping.

She cursed her husband. 'You are sitting there watching. My water has been stolen.'

Her husband looked at her.

'You are going mad,' he told her. 'You are nearing menopause, do you know?'

They had no space for an open well. And they had no money anyway.

* * *

Ramanathan Junior is lolling in his single bed. There is oil in his hair and teenage thoughts in his head. A poster of Freddie looms over him. One leg is in the air and the other is on its toes. He marvels at his taut body and his luxuriant moustache.

'I should be in Bombay,' he says aloud. 'It is a place for dosti.'

He is writing an essay on the next World War. According to him water will cause a war in the next decade, not oil. He is tired of working the hand pump every day. Tankers have raised their rates and are unaffordable and he has to pump water twice a day. He walks up to his father.

'You should pay me some pocket money for all this work,' he tells him.

He watches the veins bulge. He hears his old man sputter.

'One more year's study; that is all I will allow you. Then you have to find your way. You will have to stand on your own feet.'

Junior shrugs. 'No sweat,' he says.

'When I was your age...' starts his dad.

'Dad,' interrupts Junior. 'Did you ever get caught for doing something?'

'No,' says Senior proudly.

'How do you respect a man,' writes Junior, 'who never ever got caught for doing something?'

* * *

'This year it will not rain,' said Ramanathan at the breakfast table.

The missus brought coffee whilst he swatted the morning mosquitoes. He killed two. 'Drowsy fellows, this current crop, they make no effort to get away.' His hands were splattered with his own blood. His wife had snorted in the meanwhile.

'You think you are a sage? You cannot even predict a cricket score.'

He tasted the brew. 'New powder?' he asked. There was a muddy look to the cuppa and he was sure there would be sediment at the bottom. 'The shopkeeper is giving you the dregs,' he complained.

Ramanathan had two issues that troubled him; one was water and the other coffee. Of course there was Junior as well who, unfortunately, was his issue.

The day dawned and like the many preceding it the sky was clear.

'There is nary a cloud nor a silver lining,' wrote Junior.

The south-west monsoon had come and gone and left the Western parts of the country reeling under heavy rains. Even Delhi had borne the brunt. For some reason Chennai got none of it. There were a few cloudy days and some thunder had promised precipitation. When the month of September came and the rain deficit yawned, the citizenry decided to appease the Gods. Just in case. Just in case the north-east monsoon also decided to play truant.

The Christian brothers started to sing in their tremulous, off-key manner to Yesu. Yagyas were held in Mylapore and smoke rose from house and temple. Clouds gathered and below them people did too. But few drops fell. The

Government thought of a cloud seeding program in October. The programme was urgent but pending. The end of that month showed up without the usual rain.

Arumugam was all aquiver. Ground water was calling him and so was the citizenry. The water tankers were all over the city plying truckloads to all takers. The bore-well diggers were busy too. Newspaper reports suggested that the water table was falling. Srihari's well was drying up and its wall had developed a crack.

* * *

'This year it will not rain,' intoned Ramanathan again in November.

His wife wanted to hit him with the broom she was holding. She was worried all the same.

Junior was in a tumescent state in this dry spell. His Nepali friend had returned to Nepal to visit his village which had seen plunder. Maoists were demanding money and eyeing his sister. Junior was venting his frustration in the YMCA gym. He followed no method but he did not lack vigour and the result was that he had started bulging in strange places.

Finally Mrs Ramanathan called the boy to the kitchen and wept. She held onto him and shed copious tears.

'It is our fault,' she cried.

She had spotted him sitting knee to knee, thigh to thigh and shoulder to shoulder with a boy. Junior was seeking love and he had found it closer home in an alleyway.

'Mother, I want to run away,' said Junior.

She held his ear and took him to his father.

'Your son has started to wear make-up,' she wailed.

'How do you know?' asked the old man. He peered at his son's face and saw only acne and a stupid grin. He sniffed and could only smell talcum powder.

The missus held out her hand. There was rouge and there was a tube of cream.

'Satisfied? Shall I show you more?'

He shook his head. The boy stood like a truant. There was no remorse, if at all there was a strange defiance. It was a vulnerable moment for him.

Ramanathan was thinking. 'Where is my horoscope?' There had to be something in the stars, after all this water thing, this muddy coffee and this gay boy cannot all troop up to him on the same day.

'Shanian,' he said finally. 'I wish I had no issue.'

The boy giggled and the sound irritated him.

* * *

Mrs Narayanan called for a meeting. In the nearby chawls lines were forming for water. Women with bright plastic vessels swayed into the path of traffic. Men looked unkempt. The city needed a good bath.

'Let us dig deep,' she urged when all had assembled. 'Let Arumugam reconfirm the spot.'

The water diviner was called again. He acted coy till the price was agreed. He came with a doubled sense of importance. The entire colony was at his beck and call. He had a good day. And he had a good look at Mrs Narayanan as she hovered around him. He stood in her midst and announced, 'Madam your water will break at 40 feet and if I go deep then again at 100 feet.'

'But,' he warned, holding up his finger. 'The stream has lost its power.'

'What is the solution for me?' asked Srihari. 'Should I deepen my well?'

This thought went down badly with the rest. This fellow Srihari had a green garden and had even installed an outdoor shower below a tree. He could be heard cavorting in the outdoor cubicle with a bar of soap.

'If you go deeper you will hit poison gas,' suggested Mrs Narayanan. The thought gave her goosebumps.

Arumugam went into a trance. He fixed a spot in Mrs Narayanan's garden and drew a circle with his wand.

'You should also do a puja,' he said.

'Puja for the bore?' asked an incredulous Mrs Narayanan.

Arumugam shook his head. 'No, madam, do a puja for rain.'

* * *

Ramanathan is right. It will not rain. Srihari's well will run dry. Saplings will sprout in it. Trees will grow in it. A bore-well will be dug in Mrs Narayanan's garden and the drill will hit rock at 150 feet. Drill bits will break and the Colony will hanker for Arumugam's blood. Subbu will lose interest in Colony matters.

'Too much infighting,' he will complain.

Junior will apply to a Film Institute near Bombay. He will pen scripts under the pseudonym 'Valiban'. And nothing much else will happen.

Valiban writes:

'Some day it will rain, of course. And that will be the end of this. And a rainbow will show up in an unlikely place.

How do I know all this?

It has happened before. The annals of this street were written before they happened.

They were.

It was a mistake, an honest mistake. Put it down to climate change. Or blame it on prescient winds that blew before the weathervane had settled. Some papers got blown away by the portent of ink to come. And a damn rainbow showed up on a Google map.'

ASHADU, ASINGHAM

Beginnings are listless for writers and lovers. Walking helps. It is a December dawn, this is a Chennai winter and watchmen here are wearing monkey caps, protecting skulls that are comfortably numb. Where the fuck is the cold? And where are my people at this hour? It is 6 a.m. and I can hear Akashwani. The signature tune thrums in my head like a morning alarm. In the nearby slum all is quiet. Things look still but they are making babies.

I go for a walk every day at this time wearing shorts and running shoes. I cross the busy Chamiers Road with care. Two cars grin as they pass by. A Pallavan Transport bus bears down on a bus stop and takes away a couple of passengers. Overhead, a plane cuts its engines as it spots some tarmac and lazily descends.

'Have you heard the price of tomatoes?' asks a passerby of another.

They buy some spinach leaves from a pushcart. The seller

sits on the cart, bow-legged and smokes a beedi. 'Keerai,' he shouts every now and then.

Morning walkers are a different breed. Some stroll, some pump their hands as they walk, a few go in groups discussing the headlines and a few overweight specimens urge themselves to walk fast, hoping to lose a kilo or at the very least appease themselves. The place reeks of sweat and deodorants. A water tanker trundles along with a full load belching smoke on the curves. An impatient taxi honks and gets shouted at. And a poosari hurtles past on a motorcycle, bearing tidings, looking every inch a messenger, a courier perhaps in today's time. His cream veshti struggles to cover his legs. His shorn head bears white marks and a red dot.

I watch them all. These are my people. In my world every life has an onlooker and every street has a stalker. In Rainbow Colony I am the one. I trawl this place with a lazy eye that dwells where I cannot. Small movements here herald my day. I sense my people before they arise. Someone is reaching out for spectacles, someone is sitting at the edge of the bed waiting for back pain to subside, one busy pestle is grinding masala, one early stone is making paste. The air carries invocation between hurried breaths, an entreaty gets stone-walled by a murti; matches are struck, one agarbatti takes flame before another and drops some ash. This stirring at dawn is a communion without faces. I walk haltingly. Traces of my breath can be found on the cars parked on the pavement. I pause next to them, unsure. The steps to each doorway call out to me and I wish I could slip into these houses; this Sharada Illam, this Saraswati Nilayam, this Brenz Villa and this bare plot that threatens to prosecute me for trespass.

Trespass I will. In my nature is weed, the kind my people smoke and the kind that climbs cenotaphs next door.

When I set out today I am half asleep. The street outside my home is a narrow stretch and yesterday's leftovers lie scattered. Dogs have upturned bins and crows have rummaged the packets. Some fallen leaves look unruly. 'This is a mongrel of a day,' I tell myself. 'This dawn will show us up.'

I meet the flower-seller on my way back. She carries a basket of threaded flowers on her head and sells hand-lengths to homes in the neighbourhood. For most of them it is a couple of hands of jasmine. She is a little touched. Twenty years of vending buds and yet no flowers adorn her hair. She has had a string of men I am told. And a line-up of babies who care for each other while she roams. I talk to her in English. She smiles her lack of understanding. 'Don't know, saar,' she says, now and then. She has a singsong way, a lilt that is curiously attractive.

'Why do I rail?' I ask her.

'Rail?'

'Why do I rail against the futility of these small lives?'

'Don't know, saar.' She shakes her head.

'I grew up with these lives,' I tell her. 'I didn't get burnt. So why am I gutted?'

She scratches her head, calling to attention her unruly hair.

'I will admit to one fascination,' I confess.

'Saar?'

'Straight men.'

She shrugs, shifting the basket from her left hip to her right.

'And I have one parting question for you.'

'Gundu malli?' she asks, offering a fat white flower which has a strong fragrance. I place it behind my ear, pirouette and revel in her confusion.

'What makes straight men so?' I ask her.

* * *

Ranga was like my elder brother. In our small group of Rainbow Colony collegians we called him Anna; he acted like an elder statesman. He was experienced in all the minor vices and rumour had it that he had laid women as well. The biggest vice in high school and college was sex. All we knew about sex was found in books. Those days the internet was yet to take hold. Sex hid between our textbooks in class, it climbed onto cinema posters that said *Raaz* or *Andheri Raat Mein*, it suggested itself in shapes like pears and sizes like 38, it resided next door amongst the neighbours' curtains and at night sex came at us relentlessly like a phantom at an opera. Sex fucked us. We were a bunch of bedwetting wimps.

Ranga was past all this and had reached a stage where he was puzzling over existential issues. Like feelings. He had questions.

'Why does sex feel different every time?'

It does?

'Where do these different feelings come from?'

We looked below.

'The wellspring is not in thy groin.'

We had no answers. We had our own share of problems. Self-administration was endemic those days; it was fun and it was better than wetting the bed and leaving telltale scars that the maid would look at or, as in my case, the mother would puzzle over.

'Have you been drinking tea in bed, kanna?'

'Yes. Yes.'

Ranga was more profound.

'It is called nightfall,' he said, between puffs of smoke. 'Nightfall is a common adolescent phenomenon amongst those who haven't experienced the real thing.'

It was a guilty pleasure, whenever it happened. In deep sleep I was aware of the coming, the onrush and the waking instinct was to prevent it or at least come to life and stop the stain on the sheet, get up, run to the washroom and clean up.

'There is only symptomatic relief,' said Ranga.

He laughed. 'The root cause of nightfall is beyond you, thambi.'

I was confused. Was this some malady?

Ranga led me to Hashmi Dawakhana, a place that caused him merriment. He showed me pills called Sikander-e-Azam, a pill for enhancement and enlargement, and Mughal-e-Azam, a pill for premature ejaculation. And he read me a portion about nightfall that he thought would help me.

The patient in dream feels that some beautiful woman is beside him, he starts doing sexual act with her and the semen is discharged. In the beginning he rises up immediately at the time of discharge but slowly he is so much in the grip of this disease that he fails to know when he has discharged semen while asleep.

'Disease? Patient?'

Fuck.

'There is a solution,' said Ranga. And he read some more.

To avoid frequent nightfall young men should not indulge in vulgar talks, see nude photographs and should not read sexual literature, which arouses their sexual feelings. Do not take hot milk at night. In the morning to walk barefoot on green grass is very helpful for those who have frequent night discharges.

Walk on green grass? Avoid hot milk? I remember my mother giving Ramanathan some hot badam milk some nights. I swear they were full moon nights.

Ranga was doubled over in laughter.

For the next few days I walked past lawns and felt the urge to remove my footwear. At night I waited for the milk to cool. But nothing changed. I was trapped. I was prey. I was caught forever between nightfall and morning dew.

Years later things had changed and yet the guilt remained. Ranga wasn't always around to help. The Act brought mixed feelings.

'Mother,' I would whisper, as I lay with a man in my bed. 'Are these beasts in my bestiary, these fabulous creatures who wander between the real and the imaginary?'

'Stay young,' says my partner as he turns over.

I wish. I wish I could preserve the first bloom of youth, the time when the world is a lark and you fritter away all that is worth preserving. There is no dawakhana for a time misspent, no Azam goli, no hakeem.

'Someday Valiban must die,' says Ranga. 'But don't be in a rush.'

When he smokes he speaks well and when I see him I know that his youthfulness will never die. He is the real Valiban. I am the nom de plume.

* * *

Rainbow Colony is a lower-middle-class Brahmin enclave. It is an urban agraharam that is feeling the pinch. You can see it in the meanness of speech for that is the first thing that suffers. Words are few here and hard on the ears. I miss gaiety. The place and its people get my goat. When I write about them I give vent.

This street is a fucking stray. Each house holds a random litter from a motherless bitch. These men are my fathers, these men are my sons. These are my fellow motherfuckers. They make me write. Their anonymous lives make me write like this.

Somewhere in this jumbled mass I have to find my space, an empty space that is my private haven. Emptiness is a quality that I aspire to. I need a place where nothing stirs, where there is a lack of feeling. A womb without purpose. A centre with no edges. A pretentious notion? No, a Ramanathan.

My parents were severely impaired. They had a Brahmin worldview. The world was their cloister. Most of my relatives were engineers. We had a large extended family in California and a few on the East Coast who had succumbed to Wall Street. There were many in my age group. First cousins, second cousins, inbred, outbound; two were my uncles and one was my niece.

'Why don't you think like us?' they asked.

Our thinking was meant to be similar. Our past was attributed to probability and our future was left to calculus.

'Consider caste as a vector and sub-caste as a sub-vector,' said my uncle. He was a Maths professor in Berkeley. 'Look at how they intersect. Zoom in. Then marriages become planned surprises.'

'Wider Choice' came from matrimony.com where a sorting algorithm took care of fringe types and marginals like me. As time went by and my profile took shape the algorithm busted me and I dropped out of the marriage market.

My mould broke in school. There was a pissing competition in Class Eight and we stood in line and peed with gusto. A baniya Agarwal goaded himself, shouting some mantra I could not comprehend. One word was dharti and another was dhara. He could piss. He slaked the thirsty earth and won. I learnt that day by simple dint of looking at my neighbours that there was no such thing as a Brahmin cock. That busted my worldview.

'Go tell your mother,' said my baniya classmate, as he shook his cock dry. 'Tell her what you saw.'

It was an important day in my life. To my left and right were better cocks. Decidedly. At that tender age this discovery opened my eyes. Nature began to present itself differently from then. Shapes and sizes were an endless source of fun. Even when my high school friends went on to obsess over mangoes, melons and mounds I was left to reflect on my phallic environment, the first stirrings of which were being felt. This furry wonder, this lund, could breathe, it had a life, it could peg a tent, tangle with nada and sometime would help someone burst into song whose crescendo would bring the house down.

My father called these things 'ashadus'. My mother thought they were 'asingham'.

Cocks have feelings. Beyond the civil construction, the mechanics, the well conceived hydraulics and all such parlance, cocks have feelings. In Mylapore near the temple mine most decidedly had a mind of its own, enthused by those that sprouted in sanctorum and those that were bathed in milk and ghee and treated as deity. It showed its wilful self. I gave it a name. Called it Myself. Myself belonged to the boy next door. His bums were buns. This was my sanctum; his ark ushered me; we floated in hell.

* * *

In my India we carry wounds. Guns are blasé, knives are infra dig. Somebody really important wrote about a wounded civilization. None of that shoddy stuff for me. I carry with me a sentence like a gangster carries a gunshot. That gunshot saved the gangster. It found his friend, his sworn enemy and a culpable bystander. My sentence deals with my vicinity in much the same way. It doesn't define me, or make me or describe my time on earth. It misses the point.

Valiban was born because an ashadu did some asingham, for no reason other than a failed condom. His father Ramanathan suffered an uncontrollable urge, swayed by the hips of a Padmini, or the lips of a Savithri or even the strewn open page of a Modesty Blaise; *he mounted Kamala in the mid of an afternoon; he paused mid-flight, a moment of pure abandon, he reached out, but he couldn't find the condoms in his mind. 'Ashadu,' said Kamala, secretly pleased. So came the lion cub, Valiban. When his cord was cut his marrow showed.*

The many faces of Valiban hide, conceal, confuse and terrorize one person: Valiban. He is a writer without a backbone, without fight but with plenty of spleen and wherewithal. He is also a Brahmin who cannot count.

* * *

I could write reams on the eroticism of the homo sapiens. Super charged stuff. The nights are long. Because fuck is an incoherent jab and sex is violence. Come to Valiban. Feed his soul. This is the wild child.

In the morning I write the truth. The essential nature of man is debasement.

Andha Naal (That day) Nyamagam (memory) Vandade (returned) Nanbane (my friend).

What the fuck.

It struck me that people who write history do so without the memory. And if the mind cannot feel what the eye has not seen then history is fiction, poetry even.

VALIBAN

AS A YOUNG MAN WHO SET OUT TO WRITE I had very little precedent. I was twenty years old, born to a placidity called Ramanathan and a career housewife called 'Engadi Irukae'. That's what he called her. If his tone was fond that meant 'Where art thou?' Most often he barked and that meant 'Where the hell are you?' My mother cooked, swabbed and swept. And she fetched. His slippers, his reading glasses, his endless glasses of water and his ointments. Fractional delays caused irritation and she would get flustered.

'Engadi Irukae?'

The sound of hurry and the dropping of something. The sound of apology.

Why was he in a hurry? He was a lazy retiree with nowhere to go. I wanted to cut through his routine. I wanted to tell him off because I feared I would grow up and become like him. This is the stock I come from, I told myself. This is the stuff I will breed.

Our house was dimly lit. Evening visitors would arrive and lament, ‘Voltage is low again.’ They did not know that my father bought sixty watt bulbs instead of hundred because that saved money. As a child I learnt to peer. I would place my finger on the page and read. Like a dimwit.

I had my own room. It was small and it had a high mirror that kept me on my toes. There was a window the size of two bricks. I had a single bed, a small fan and a calendar that was five years old. I liked that calendar and couldn’t let go. It had Shiva in an animal skin. Old calendars are confusing. Days of the week arrived as surprises.

‘Today is Saturday, isn’t it?’

‘You have no respect for Monday,’ shouts Ramanathan. Monday was the first day of the week for the office-goer. You had to bow to it.

‘Get up I say.’

Obeisance is a shave and a shower and a shirt with fewer creases.

‘Hurry up, you will miss the bus.’

No time for breakfast today and no time for a look in the mirror.

‘Tuck your shirt in. You are going in those chappals?’

As I leave I get under his skin.

‘Find me a thambi,’ I tell him.

‘What? Find a thambi? You think you get brothers in the T. Nagar market?’

I count my bus money.

‘I am an only child. I have to take all your shouting.’

At the bus stop I kept my patience by counting vehicle numbers. The ones that added up to seven were mine. I was in a hurry to live my life. I needed fodder to write. I wanted to compress my growing years. The pace at home was a drag and inspiration was hard to find. I needed to finish my English Literature degree and get away. Yet I was a reluctant graduate. They had to drag me to the university exams with threats of starvation. For me starvation meant no cigarettes and no alcohol. At the examination hall I kept winking at the invigilator. It was a tic brought on by withdrawal.

'Ennada porriki?' he whispered into my ear. 'Are you *that* type?'

I was.

Porikki I wasn't. Though I had the habits of a vagabond.

I lapse into Tamil now and then. It is the only language that makes sense sometimes. For when I walk the roads of the city the urban slum is never far behind. There are queues for water and queues for the public toilet. And mornings are pressing moments. Cuss words come. The men stand on the side and brush their teeth or scratch their shorts that lie below veshtis. The women fight. It must be a hard life for they curse so well. They tear each other by the hair and their voices change tone. The tired harridans curse till the last word is claimed. The men hide and I blush.

I like Tamil crude. I like how it sounds. For example: Let us examine your short hair. That sounds simple; delicate even. The way I say it: Mayira pudingi. That grabs you by the short hair.

My college was a city college. It was also called a day college. We had a large campus full of beautiful buildings that were planted there from another time. I and my friends did not belong to this vision. We were there because the tuition fee was very cheap, the car park would rest bums for free and the canteen gave dosai on credit. I spent most of my time in the cavernous library.

College also kept us away from home. I decided to surprise my parents once by coming home early. I had cinema tickets for a matinee.

'Pokiri has been sent home,' said the father. 'Were you smoking beedis in class?'

'Charminar, dad. I do not smoke beedis.'

'Same thing.'

Pokiri, porikki; take your pick. Everybody loafed at my age in an under-graduate arts programme.

I spent three years in my college and nothing untoward happened. There was a world outside that I knew existed. It was a vast and complex system and I wanted no part of it. I learnt a few things in college. I learnt that I could be completely irrational. I stood for the student leader election in my third year. I made my first true enemy.

My father was horrified when he got to know.

'Leader? Are you a communist porikki?'

All college leaders were trouble-makers and lefties.

'Ramanathan,' I reproached him.

'You called me by name?' This was riposte.

'Remember the name: Ramanathan,' I replied. I said it like I did in college.

I was getting good at introducing myself.

'What happens if you lose?' asked Ramanathan.

This was a question that ruled his life. He had spent a lifetime covering his backside.

'Losing helps, Dad,' I replied.

* * *

I sat at the college bus stop and I wrote election posters. At the same time I was scripting my failure as well.

I sent my election poster to my father. It exalted courage among students. It was written in a mixture of coarse Tamil and classic English; written when I was charged up with the better half of a Napoleon Brandy. The failed Frenchman was coursing in my blood and eking out English.

I urged the students to unite behind me against Pandian. Pandian was a Madurai Veeran. Or so he said. I knew better.

'He is a border case from Palghat,' shouted the poster.

'He is a history-sheeter, did you know?' it headlined.

'The Police Station in nearby Aminjakarai has his mug shot on an FIR,' it informed.

The more I railed and revealed the more votes I lost. I listed Pandian's failings and I signed off as I usually did.

'Who is this Valiban who has written to me?' asked my father. 'And who is this Pandian?'

'Pandian is a thevadiya pillai,' I muttered.

He is who I am up against in the election.

I lost the election. Pandian beat me by a country mile.

He spread a rumour in the college that I was gay. He said he had a certificate to prove it. He plastered the number nine on every tree and lamppost in the college with my mug shot in it. There is slang in Tamil that says 'Ombodu'. That's who I was; a castrated son of a bitch. The smear campaign worked.

I wept for the first time in my life when I lost the election. For me that was an irrational thing to do. I mean why? When you lose publicly you change. The smear campaign branded me for life as a gay. I wasn't ready for it.

'Ramanathan,' I tell my dad. 'I have lost my virginity.'

His nerves well up and his eyes bulge.

'Where? I mean with whom?'

'Don't ask,' urges the mother. She could make a wild guess.

'Preposterous,' he says finally. His English surprises me sometimes.

'Insolent fellow, you are my blood I say.' He pauses and then cannot help using the slang he wanted to. 'Bastard.' There, it was out of his system. 'Bastard,' he repeats.

'What have I done to deserve this?'

He looks at my mother. 'Where did we go wrong?'

She looks at the sky with her hands held high.

I think we are all caricatures, cardboard cut-outs who mouth the same dialogue.

'Dad,' I pipe up. 'Can you lend me some money?'

It was better to ask him before he copped it. I needed to leave the city. I needed a change of scene.

* * *

Mumbai treats me kindly. It has me in a tight embrace. It keeps me close to its beating heart. And it sends me home. I have a set of memories in sequence that start with dirt and end with song. The place is a pit, a vast teeming pit. In it are people who do not know it. They do not look sideways, they do not look up. They turn their backs on it to catch the setting sun or the falling rain. My interview was in a place called Kalina. Kalina is a nowhere land between Kurla in the East and Santa Cruz in West Mumbai. It is a place where I would shoot a gritty Western.

Mumbai is a place for gritty films. It is all there, the

setting, the life, the daily spectacle; I am aghast at the candyfloss and confetti that its films throw up.

I walk into a ramshackle structure which used to be a factory. I open the door and inside is sheen, glass and chrome. Lighting comes from the floor and the ceiling; the walls are busy with posters. The floor is metal. This for me is where I belonged. I wanted it bad, suddenly. Things went badly. I did not have the look. If at all, I stood out for the wrong reasons. If only they would let me talk.

They started with a list.

'Any special skills?' None.

'Have you held a camera before?'

'No. I have stood for election and I have written posters.'

They look at a couple that I have submitted. Coarse Tamil finds no echo in their eyes.

'I lost the election,' I inform them. 'Isn't that worth something?'

This isn't going well.

Should I tell them I have imagination, belief and cunning?

'Any family business?' No.

'Are you ambitious?' I was.

'Say something ambitious.'

'I want to write a colloquial film. It will be set in Chennai.'

'We are not sure you are ready for a film writing course.'

'Why?'

'Your self-image and your skill sets are... how should we say this?'

'Don't.'

I so wanted to say something to change their mind. They had ruffled my papers and moved on to the next profile.

On the train ride back to Chennai, I sat desolate and thought. What is it I wanted to do?

I wanted to write stuff that children could not read. My stories were meant to be read between the pages of textbooks in class. They were to be hidden under pillows at home. They were to be torn out from their binding and shared in toilets. Bad language was not enough to make this grade.

I would make a film that would be banned. It would be seen by the underground. It would be pirated with my consent.

* * *

I had an encounter in Mumbai. That is what I went for. The thing about Mumbai is that it has no preamble. I suspect foreplay doesn't exist or at least it is nearing extinction. I saw foreplay on the parapet walls of the marinas, I saw sweaty play in the back seats of taxis and I saw it in the corner seats of cinema halls. The onlookers looked excited and exchanged smiles even. There was no clucking at this public display. This is wrong, I said to myself. Where is the meeting of eyes? This was all hands. This was furtive stuff. The combatants were past caring.

The place where my encounter happened was a mess. It was a by-lane. And people swore there was love in that by-lane. If so it was a hardy creature that reared itself. Ramanathan's house would cost a king's ransom in this seedy place. I walked through a door into another door, then a small windowless corridor into a waiting room that had two intimate seats. A tubelight shone on a scenic wallpaper and the smell from the pantry was of stale tea.

My date was late and the excuse was a train. We sat next

to each other and spelt awkward. And then we wandered into the dark.

We spent all of half an hour. I fumbled. I could write a tome on fumbling in the dark. The conversation was inane, the sounds carried and my mind asked questions even as the ministrations were very good. The fellow cleaned up like a professional.

I cancelled my two other dates and I preponed my ticket to Chennai.

'What happened?' asked my mother. 'Why are you returning early?'

What should I have told her? I was confused about the city.

This place is a bad romance, I felt. A four-letter word like love needs nourishment. People here live in square feet. I need space that has no purpose. I need to look around with time on my hands. I need to stand and contemplate in a public space. People here had bells on their feet. They were constantly being shepherded.

I hated the word gritty by then. Within two days of walking the streets of Mumbai I had grit in my nose. Poetry here is gritty, said a magazine. People here overcome, said a newspaper. 'Excuse me,' I asked. 'Where do I dig my nose?'

My mother was still on the line.

'I feel like an outsider,' I told her.

She sounded happy.

* * *

'Ramanathan,' I whisper.

The old man wakes with a start. He reaches for his spectacles. He looks for his bedside time-piece. It is 4 a.m.

'Porikki,' he shouts. 'What are you doing here?'

'I am back.'

As an announcement it did not move the Richter scale. But it was close.

'Are you lucid?' I ask.

He aims a swipe and almost dislocates a shoulder. His palm chops a tumbler.

He has forgotten that I have a name.

'You? What are you doing here?'

'Tell me about your childhood.'

I have pen and paper. I have brought his morning coffee. He catches sight of it and this act of mine floors him. He swallows a curse, pulls himself up and stumbles to the toilet. I can hear the creak of bone joints.

He returns quickly, pulls the tumbler from the dabra, throws his head back and pours the hot brew down his throat. I swallow in reflex. It is good coffee. I can make out. The old man is close to orgasm. He adjusts his veshti, smoothens his poonal and runs a comb through his hair. Something in the mirror is not right. He grimaces and gestures towards the verandah.

It is dark outside and very quiet. Ramanathan Senior is having a senior moment. He is quite disoriented.

'So you missed the train?' he begins.

'I boarded it and stepped off.'

He digests this with difficulty. I can hear him calculate the cancellation charges even as he is guessing why I have returned.

'Dad, that was two days ago. I attended the interview and they rejected me. Today is Wednesday.'

'Kanna,' he says finally. And he says no more for a while. He looks old.

'I have to write a screenplay, Ramanathan. I have to write it on someone who I know well and yet haven't understood.'

'Today is Wednesday?' He looks at his watch. He shakes his head vigorously. 'Two days have passed since you went for the interview?'

I nod.

'Where is your mother?'

'In the kitchen, where else?'

'So Bombay threw you back?' He cannot help a 'I thought so' snigger. I try to steer him to my pressing need.

'My screenplay is on someone who has lived a life that nobody knows about. It is about small moments. It is about a street that is not on anybody's map.'

'Have you had a bath in the last two days? You look like a rowdy.'

I persevere. I am sure the back of his mind is registering something.

'It will be a throwback to the olden day scripts. Forget today's heroes, superstars and supermen. We need you, Ramanathan. You are an anti-hero. There are no villains save in your head. You have no issues except me. And your wife does for you all her life without questioning her own worth.'

Bingo.

'What was that last thing you said?'

'My script will search for redemption. It will dig deep for meaning. It will cut through the stasis you are steeped in, the quagmire and the...'

The old man has stood up. He is profiled against a

streetlight. I decide right then that this will be in black and white. I will write without colour.

'You are not a zero, Ramanathan. Nobody is. And that is the triumph. If I can make a script out of your life it will be the miracle my life needs.'

I watch with concern as he steps up to me. I am still seated.

'You turned out different, right. From this house came you. Is that not a better story? What made you happen?'

He is asking himself. He needs a simple answer, preferably one that pointed away from him and one that he could reverse.

'Act 1: Take 1,' I announce. 'Ramanathan, are you ready?'

'Ready?'

'How will you die? I will let you choose.'

'Die, so soon?'

* * *

The day after my father's death dawned, I slept in his room, in his bed. I woke up amidst his possessions. And for a day I looked up his life. The day took an age to end, time moved slowly and the little things of routine became reasons to pass time. This pace would kill me in a week. Evening brought the realization that this was a small life. Was it less lived? Had Ramanathan done justice to his time on earth?

I spent the evening clearing his chest of drawers. I found sundries, middle-class undies and a copy of the Ramayana. His cupboard had cuttings from newspapers, photographs and accounting statements. In a frayed file were his tax returns. In a corner of his cupboard I uncovered a couple of my school essays. And I found a bunch of letters that hadn't been posted. It was a thick bunch wrapped with strings and rubber bands. Each letter was written by hand. The first was on the day I was born. The last on the day I left for Mumbai. I read the letters through the night. Beautiful letters, heartfelt words, canny observations, and here and there the spirit of sorrow mingled with regret. Letters to a son.

Mayiru pudingi. The old man had forgotten his will but left me the testament.

WHITE LIES

SOMEBODY DEAD IS STALKING ME. Somebody I used to know very well. He leaves cotton threads on my bed and grey hair on my floor.

There is a photograph of him on my wall. It has a garland of dry flowers around it. Every day it tilts to a side and I have to straighten it.

I catch Thangavel when he is escaping. He is a breezy fellow and he disappears in a flash. When it is 6 p.m. the door to his cabin opens cautiously, he peeps out, looks left first and then right, and then he tiptoes to the back door. Irate applicants like me are known to prowl in his office. His peon has already brought his two-wheeler to the rear entrance.

To be fair, he always has time for you when you catch hold of him. Like I have. Just as he is about to kick-start his scooter I latch on to his umbrella. It is an old style umbrella and it opens as I grab it. We have a stand off.

I am holding his umbrella and he is tugging.

'Garu,' he exclaims, as if he has discovered me after many years.

'Ramanathan,' I correct him. 'G. Ramanathan. Son of now deceased S. Ramanathan.'

'Of course, of course. I know that. You look like an Andhra landlord.'

I looked harried, I am sure.

'My umbrella,' he says.

I am still holding it and I am not letting go, yet.

'I tried to meet you yesterday. I was waiting outside your office day before, and last week I warmed the bench outside your cabin till they offered me a job.'

He smacks his head with his palm and clucks loudly.

'Garu, I was so busy. Today is my first day in office after a week.'

'You were in your cabin all the time,' I say doggedly.

'Of course not, how could I be in two places at the same time?'

'Exactly,' I reply. The umbrella is now in my secure custody.

He owes me an explanation and I give him time to manufacture something good that will save my pride.

'Am I a ghost?' he asks.

He laughs anxiously.

'Sir, I really think your ghost was in your cabin all these days. I saw files go in, I saw rubber stamps falling on paper and I saw signatures on the files that came out.'

He scratches his tummy.

'Your file number ends with 7, correct? And the total of the file number adds up to 7, correct?'

'Yes.' I have to agree.

'You see, I remember. It is on the top of my mind,' he proclaims.

'Sir, it is one month since I applied.'

The man lies through his teeth. I know when this man is lying; he is not even thinking about what he is saying.

He places a hand on my shoulder.

'The matter is under process,' he says.

He grabs his umbrella and he is gone.

The next day he forwards the file. I am seated outside and Thangavel's ghost has signed it.

'Saar will definitely come tomorrow,' says the peon. 'Then you can meet him.'

All I wanted to do was thank him this time.

* * *

Somebody who is stalking me should be dead. There is a trace of his breath on the morning mirror. There is writing on the dusty windows of my small car.

My file moved from Thangavel the Ghost to his boss, Bhatia the Shadow.

Bhatia is a senior officer. He has paled. His family treats him like a shadow.

One day he sat alone in his bedroom and pulled out all his papers. He saw his degree certificate and his mark sheets. He saw the centum in maths, the eighty in history and the pass mark in science. Each paper was a story.

Bhatia came from good middle stock. His father was a government servant and his mother a teacher. They stayed in the Gol Market area in Delhi, a place famous for food items and the Birla Mandir. Their flat was small and young Bhatia studied wherever he found space. He studied hard to make up for a modest intelligence. He had good retentive power and weak eyesight. He never played any sport.

Bhatia's childhood friend was a dog. The dog left him.

After his schooling marks came out his father went to work looking for quotas. There were none that he fitted into. Admissions were difficult. Finally, one day that everybody remembers, the young boy got admitted to a BSc Programme in an ethnic sounding college. That day sweetmeats got made in the Bhatia house. The gas cylinder was overworked and it burst. The flat caught fire and the fire engines came to clear the debris and save the neighbours. The Bhatia family stood outside holding his admission card.

Bhatia felt that somebody was not looking out for him. He had to wear the same clothes for his first week in college.

BSc lead to MSc. The boy had a lot of spare time. He became a crammer. He learned by rote anything he could lay his hands on. The house they moved into had a library somebody left behind. There were books and more books.

Then came the Civil Services Exam and Bhatia sat for them. The years of cramming helped and the boy got into a minor service. They posted him by turns to all the extremities of the country, wherever trouble erupted. Each time his boss was a South Indian. Each time he suffered.

Bhatia felt nobody up there was looking out for him.

Marriage was followed by children; two of them, one boy and one girl. After this the wife retired from his company. He had nothing to offer that she found exciting. She found rummy among friends a diversion and the studies of her children more important. Some days she forgot he was there. He was there every day after 7 p.m. He would sit in the corner of the living room and read history books and biographies. He belonged to the company of great men and significant events.

Bhatia's looks changed so much that one day he went to the doctor after spying himself while shaving.

'Where is the blood?' he asked the doctor.

He looked pale, his nails were pale, his eyes were rheumy and when he scratched himself badly all he saw was white skin that had split.

'Where is the blood?' he repeated.

The doctor drew some blood, thankfully. Bhatia took the vial home. He watched the colour change.

Bhatia is a shadow. The sun determines his shape and size. Once it sets he retires.

In his office, papers came to him in the IN tray. They basked there for a while till somebody made noise. Then he saw them. Pulls and pressures worked on Bhatia. Somebody needed to toggle him. If the papers were South Indian he moved them slowly.

I did not know that. So I sat outside his office like I did with Thangavel. My file stayed for a long time in the IN tray. Till I barged in. And I asked reasons for the delay.

'There is no delay,' said Bhatia. 'Who told you?'

'You cannot move things faster?' I shouted.

The pale shadow spoke and it lied. 'It is not in my hands.'

I had heard this before. I told him his longevity was in my hands. I could not believe what I was saying. I told him if he did not move that piece of paper he would be reduced to one that belonged in his bloody office.

'Bloody?' he asks.

'Yes, bloody.'

I seem to have hit a chord. That day I discovered that shadows could sign.

* * *

The house that I stay in had an untimely death. When that happens things take time to settle down. I wish people looked me in the eye. They think I am hiding something. They think I am responsible in some way.

I was on the last lap. I needed just one more signature. The boss supremo of this government dump was Chockalingam. I had been told to watch out for him. He was a shrewd officer and he wasn't lazy.

Chockalingam liked paruppu podi. He carried the powder wherever he went. I knew because I sat there during his lunchtime. His dabba would steam past and I would imagine his rice, his ghee and his podi. The fellow made a drama about eating. In would go his ever-silver thali, his spoon and tumbler and then his tiffin carrier.

For the next half an hour there would be a metal cacophony. Chockalingam was a noisy eater. He would emerge with his hands dripping and rush to the washroom. A loud gargle and some spirited spitting would follow. He would then come and stand in front of me and smile.

'Have you brought all the details?' he would ask, wiping his hands on a small hand towel.

And I would hand over all the obscure information he had asked for.

'In those times nobody kept any information,' he would remark as he studied the papers. 'You needed a good tehsildaar.'

After a quick perusal the customary remark that I dreaded, 'This is missing. What you have given me is valuable but it is better if you can trace this also.'

I made three trips to our family village and one to my father's childhood town. I bent and scraped my way in front of people who welcomed me with gusto. They apologized often for they could not always help.

I have a stamina for most things. This episode tested me to the full. Finally I had to throw my hands up because record-keeping in the days gone by was very poor. I went up to Chockalingam before his lunch arrived. He looked hungry and surprised.

'What you are asking for, what if I cannot get it?'

He thought.

'It is not compulsory,' he said.

I could not believe what I was hearing.

'And what I gave you the last three times?'

'Not compulsory,' he repeated.

I felt a suffocation. I could have hugged him to death.

'Then why did I have to go through all this?'

'Why were you in a hurry?' asked Chockalingam.

Why was I? Why was I chasing this piece of paper?

The next day it was official. Ramanathan Senior had died. It went on record. The signed death certificate was in my hands.

I took it home, stood in front of the photograph and displayed it. The damn thing fell; the photo frame fell to the floor and broke some clichés. I left it there.

The next morning I blew moisture on my mirror and wrote my father's name. And I watched it disappear. I was done.

People said later that the office that issued death certificates changed, after I left. People began to shun it, saying it was haunted. The watchmen swore they saw an old man hunting for papers every night.

I was not surprised.

VII

MURTHY

NULLAH

SENIOR INSPECTOR MURTHY IS A BURLY MAN who conveys gravity. Every step of his is measured and he chooses his words carefully. On days when the sun is out he absorbs light by merely standing at the entrance of his Police Station in full view, trying it would seem, to scare crime away. The neighbourhood was clearly rattled by this show of force. Roughnecks moved to other suburbs, it is rumoured.

Murthy carries the world on his burly shoulders and a Taj on his head. One day I shook up his world. Believe me, it takes a lot to shake a cop like Murthy. For all his easy-going airs and unaffected nature he had a soft spot for kids. Make that a blind spot. He had no children of his own.

I had a difficult week. I showed him two children. Both found on a railway track just three days apart. It was not pretty, the look on Murthy's face. I had taken him there because something about the two incidents did not make sense.

The railway track skirted the southern portion of Rainbow Colony like a hemline. There was a broad gauge track and a narrower suburban track. The portion of track where these incidents occurred was on a narrow raised bund. There was a mud pathway on each side that was used for carts and people walked on them all the time. On the other side of the track was a nullah; a small dirty stream with some greenish flow. You had to wade through it to get to the pathway on the other side or try to jump on the misshapen stone boulders that had been placed in the water for people to get across. There was a sharp bend in the track a few yards down around which were some pottikadais, shops that sold all manners of things.

We had a hard time with the families of the two children. They thronged the cop station. Why? I don't know. They had to go somewhere, catch someone and say something. Murthy was not good at this and so he kept to himself in his room. I met up with the throng and spent hours listening to them and pretending to write down whatever they said. It was a terrible experience. By the weekend I was having difficulty sleeping. Murthy never spoke a word all week.

That weekend we decided to visit the spot. We couldn't just close the file. It would have been easy to mark the facts, file the photographs and build up an accident case. But I wanted to show some effort to the families and Murthy agreed to come along.

'Something doesn't add up, sir,' I told him as we got going.

He nodded. 'Exactly what I was thinking; nothing happens in twos,' he said.

We took a detour to attend some obligatory functions.

There were two that evening that we had to attend. One was a show of photographs by a Police Commissioner. This senior officer travelled frequently and carried his camera with him. He had captured sunrises and sunsets, rivers, boats, seas, locals at a fishing village or just any village, street shots from the city and just about anything that caught his fancy. Somebody told him he had a gift and that his photographs were truly museum quality. Promptly a number of them got printed and framed and an exhibition date was taken at a prominent gallery.

The second function was a show of paintings by the wife of a General in the Army. These were landscapes from the countryside and paintings of groups of women at a well, in the field, outside their huts and a couple of paintings had them walking into the sunset.

Two such exhibitions in the same day and Murthy and I were hard-pressed to stay calm. We had walked around the two shows, had cups of tea and made small talk.

'Nothing happens in twos,' I said and Murthy snorted.

His face had a curious expression. I realized he wanted to say something but could not find the right words. I escaped into the washroom where I spent a long time combing my hair. When I returned Murthy was still viewing and making encouraging noises. Finally when we left and reached the jeep he wiped his glasses after blowing into them and said 'Why?'

We visited the Railways office later in the evening. They had sent a team to review the spot to try and understand what happened. They drew a blank. Sure there was a bend in the track, both the incidents happened at the twilight hour and the trains were moving fast. But the sound and vibrations would awaken even a sleeping child leave alone an alert one.

We asked some more questions. They got defensive.

'Please understand that this wasn't a regular railway crossing. Right? And the track was clearly elevated. You had to climb to reach it, sir.'

'The place needs a crossing,' mumbled Murthy.

'We cannot have a crossing for every mile,' said the supervisor. 'Yes, there are slum settlements on both sides. But a few hundred yards down we have built an underpass for them. Why cannot they use it?'

'And those pottikadais are also clearly illegal,' piped up his assistant.

We left the office promising to get back with some suggestions.

Murthy was looking for some vibrations. He had by now a familiar look; all alert and nowhere to go. We knew the families would not go away so we decided to meet them in their houses. A really bad idea.

* * *

It takes us a while to get to the first house. The lanes in the locality are narrow and the by-lanes are a squeeze. We rattle up to the house in our jeep. All is quiet and we can sense that everyone is in waiting. Yes, after the wailing gets done the waiting begins. Poor families sit around and wait. For what? I don't know, don't ask me.

After a few soft words Murthy asks some questions. Some children have crowded around us by now. The child's father is brooding in the corner and the mother speaks slowly at first and then breaks into a swaying sob. We quickly exit and move on to the next call. For this we have to cross the track. We decide to walk to get a sense of the exact location. By now the children are following our every move. Most are in sparse, torn outfits. Many are dribbling at the nose and sneezing. As we near the tracks the younger ones fall back but one fellow lingers on.

'Peyer ennai? What is your name?' asks Murthy.

'Thambi sir, oru pena.' He says, all in one breath.

'What?' asks Murthy. 'Why does he ask me for a pen?'

'If you have a pen to spare then give it to him. They all ask for one pen.'

Murthy stops and looks around. It is an open area with scattered brush and strewn urban trash. The track can be seen trailing in from a distance and as you climb up and reach it a fresh breeze blows into your face. The kids stay back now and are kicking some tins around in a football game. We eye the nullah and the slush warily and look for a shallow crossing. Halfway across we give up on our shoes and splash into the embankment. Thambi has followed us.

The second house is more of the same. By now it is getting to Murthy but he plods back the way we came. This time around he is sniffing like an anxious dog. He walks up to the kids and chats for a while. Some paint has spilt from the football cans and the grass has picked up some interesting hues. But Murthy sees none of this. He just stands around and sniffs. As does Thambi. He is sniffing one of the paint cans.

Some lawyers meet us at the office when we return. They are trying to help out the families, they say. Murthy is curt and factual and they leave after a few minutes.

'Who are they suing?' I ask.

'The Railways, who else? It seems that with so many people on both sides of the tracks there should have been some safety measures. A local politician is also getting involved.'

I lose track of the case and the files gather dust. For some reason Murthy refuses to close the case and be done with it. The legal cases finally hit the court at the familiar lethargic pace and in the meanwhile an overbridge project commences in the exact same location. In a few months time the cases get thrown out and a stray article gets written on an inner page. Murthy sends a cheque from the Police Fund.

'Should we close this file?' I ask him. He thinks for a moment and agrees. Neither of us is very satisfied but then we had no reason to pursue it any further.

The overbridge finally gets ready and the local politician is to inaugurate it with some fanfare. The railway supervisor remembers to invite us. He wants to make a point.

Murthy and I happen to visit the gallery again en route to the function. He is in a philosophical mood and strolls around silently. I watch a spider climb the wall. As we are ready to leave he sniffs.

'I love the smell of paint and varnish,' he says.

Some of the paintings still look wet and I keep my distance.

We reach the site of the bridge where a crowd has gathered. The politico is late and people mill around staring at the press who are holding cameras with long snouts. Murthy walks away and I follow him a few hundred yards off to a familiar site. The site where it all had happened. A boy comes running up to us.

'How are you, sir?' he says in perfect English. It is Thambi.

'Where do you stay?' asks Murthy.

The kid mumbles an approximate address. I notice now that he has an athletic build and keen eyes.

'Who do you stay with?' asks Murthy.

'My uncle,' he replies. He is holding a paint thinner can in his hand. He fumbles with it and drops it. Murthy bends and picks up the can. He thrusts it under my nose. The harsh smell hits me and I pull my head back. Murthy laughs as he chucks it into the nullah. I feel woolly and light-headed. It is strong stuff. It is also strangely addictive.

'Do you like this?' he asks me but looks at Thambi.

'Yes, sir,' says Thambi.

I stare at the kid. He seems to be telling the truth. I stare into the nullah at my reflection in the green, still mass and shake my head. I swivel and look into the distance. I find the horizon behind a clump of trees and spot a train in the distance snaking in. Murthy thrusts another tin under my nose and for a while I stumble along the tracks in a daze. We head back to the gathering as a train thunders past behind us. Thambi follows us like a dog that's found a friend.

UTHAMA PUTHIRAN

AND WHILE THE WORLD WAS LIVING in fear of ex-cons these released convicts were mere distractions. Nobody took notice of this ex-cop. His name was Gangadharan. Police records show his place of origin as Maduravoyal, a suburb in Chennai where dreams festered and reality failed. 'PLOTS FOR SALE' boards enticed the unwary to Maduravoyal. There were no amenities there. Water and electricity were scarce and sewage was often visible. This was the suburban way.

Gangadharan's pasture was a southern suburb called Nanganallur. This suburb had many temples with long, unpronounceable names. One such temple lost its lingam to a washerman who shifted it to a pond and used it as a stone to wash his clothes. The other gods fled, clambered to safety up the temple gopuram and looked down upon the blissful chaos of Nanganallur. Below, there was no benediction but a frown a day from elderly Brahmins who had spent their life and retired from smiling.

Gangadharan was a rowdy in the Police Force. His uniform could not contain him. He grew up on streets that brooked no pavements and houses that brooked no boundary walls; even rubbish in his locality broke free of bins. In short, Ganga was like his neighbourhood, an encroachment.

This cop thrived in precincts like Nanganallur that had low income migrants and drifters. They were easy prey. He thrived on their uncertainty. As a cop he was on the make; he became a fixer and an enforcer and eked out a stash of small currency. He came cheap and he hoped that kept him out of sight.

His wife gave him away. Nobody knew other than her. She made an anonymous call to Senior Inspector Murthy. She whispered and she wept. She hoped perhaps they would take him away to the Central Jail and feed him to the crows.

Gangadharan was asked to leave. The build up to his removal was long and excruciating; the termination order when it came was cryptic and Senior Inspector Murthy carried it like it was a brahmastra and served it to Gangadharan with relish. Murthy swore he saw his head roll and he heard temple bells ring.

* * *

This is Gangadharan. This is a movie starring him. This is him staring at you from a gigantic movie poster on Mount Road. Come down the Anna flyover and look right. There above the Church Park School he towers larger than life. Poster painters have given him a swarthy look. They have captured his likeness.

Gangadharan likes this image of himself and he likes his

drink and after a few drinks he likes to imagine a king-size version of himself; one that is taller and without his pot belly. He finds his home a depressing come down from this world; he tries to eradicate it every evening.

His household was not becoming. He transported himself through cinema. He watched a film every day; usually a Tamil film and one that had a male protagonist who he imagined wore his colours and stripes. In his imagination he was a leader of men and the chief of the community; a Kamal Haasan in Virumaandi or a Shivaji Ganesan in Thevar Magan. After a few years of an alcoholic existence his reality was a hazy rendition of what he saw at the movies. Nights he dreamt of a mansion, standing in the balcony while the caste keepers and the community stood at the turnstiles looking up to him. It did not matter if they were Gounders, Thevars or even bleeding Brahmins.

The only way he could live this fantasy at home every day was by quelling his household and denying his wife, his son and his daughter a voice.

* * *

I am a sixteen-year-old boy trapped in the body of a ten year old. I have no sense of the real world. If the real world is a window view then it exists. There is another world that exists in my home, an interior world where two civilizations collide. I study under my mother's tutelage. She teaches me the English way, a path that she feels will one day lead me out of this black hole that my father represents. She deals with me in the hours he is away. The day passes learning English. Then my father comes home. And we have a rerun of my worst nightmares brought to celluloid by a man I have learnt to fear and hate. My dad's name should have been Veerumandi. He is a man in a veshti who finds fallow compensation at home for what life has wreaked on him. He has been dealt a poor hand, he feels.

Nobody in this world knows about us. I stay at home because I cannot move much. My mother's world is domestic and my younger sister is still in junior school.

* * *

The man, who saw the movies, drank in their honour. His sense of drama was an ode to the Tamil films he saw. The sensibility was violent.

He drank brandy; not the refined cognac but merely a certified chemical. This was a land that named people after Stalin and called a brandy Napoleon. Napoleon is a bottle that yields an amber fluid that people drank till they slurred. Perhaps they should have washed it down with a soda called Waterloo.

Gangadharan's celluloid sense was this. The first peg he drank out of respect. It was ingested standing, one hand on the balcony railing, watching the night. It was called a Muthal Mariyadai.

The second was a friend of the first, a flirtatious pour that was called a Thozhi. She, and it was always a she, brought with her a licence, a laxity of purpose and a loosening of tongue. It was the time to shout for snacks and volley some abuse. 'Vaadi Kazhuthai,' he would yell. This wasn't a film title but the call to the wife, the clichéd sufferance who had to be an ass to endure his ways. By this time Gangadharan the man was on the sofa in front of the television, the remote resting on his belly, his eyes reddening by the minute.

The third drink was a challenge; it brought with it a sliver of enlightenment and a promise of violence, much like a sharp crescent moon three days in the making. You could call it a Moondram Pirai. His mind would be free by now. He could take on anything and anybody.

The fourth and after were mayhem, of the kind that every film out of the Madurai gene pool graphically portrayed. Thickset men under the influence and under the illusion that they were heroic, manic minds who spoke with knives and aruvaals wreaking havoc on near and dear out of whimsy, outdated principle and convenience. Fuck up was he needed a cause to cut loose and he often had none.

There were two eternals nearby that drew his attention; his invalid son whom he considered a blot from his loins, and that harbinger of bad luck to this lifetime, his wife.

* * *

You had to be lucky to have a house like mine. I guess I should say home as it was not a bungalow but a flat on the third floor. I had a name for it: Four Quarters. I liked the sound of that name. It is just that every day of my blessed life I would watch my moods unfurl through the windows. There were three windows where I spent my time, each opening out on to a different street, in a different direction. I remember when I was taken to a glitzy shop for my first watch; I chose one without any numbers. Just a nice dial and these arms pointing like a compass: north south east west. Four quarters. It was all I ever needed.

My father drinks alcohol. On a bad day he has four quarters.

Daybreak was my good time. I always awoke with a start.

Not because of some alarm but because the sun would light up my eyes nice and early. I always opened the curtains at night before I slept. The night breeze and night sounds would help me sleep. In Rainbow Colony there is no sea breeze. Sea breeze got diverted at the Adyar signal.

I liked to feel weather on my skin. I liked climate that I could wear.

When the sun was rising to its highest point I would be at the street-side window, watching. Is all I really needed, a little imagination and a busy street going about living a life. This is why I liked weekends. I would have a full day of goings-on to keep track of. My mother fretted at these simple pursuits and worried for my future. She thought I had aged before my time, or was a little touched. But she couldn't argue with my high school grades. I was on the English honour list. I could write like Shakespeare and read like Tennyson.

And then when the light started to fade I needed to get on to the balcony and mark time. The blues in the sky would deepen, colouring the fading reds till night fell like ink from a bottle.

And then my father would come home. And draw every curtain, every night, without fail. And hell would break loose. He would throw my English textbooks around. 'Look outside!' he would shout. 'Look at the sky. Tamil is bleeding.'

The rains completed my picture. Seasonal rains, making up for months of absence. It would come at us in sheets. And we would put up shades, tarpaulins, coats of tar and what have you. But we could never keep it out. We would start by gradually closing the windows till we tightened them shut. Yet the trickle would start from the edges and from wherever else. And a nice puddle would build up where the slopes converged. I would wait for the let-up in the rain and then throw open the windows to dangle my feet on some puddles and feel the light spray on my face. Like I said, you had to be lucky to be in Four Quarters.

My father hated the rains and the seeping water that made its way in. He said that it was an unwanted intruder, sneaking into his life, like my mother. He did slip and fall on a puddle one rainy night. We left him there, a dead drunk deadweight. The next day there was a storm.

* * *

Murthy is picking his teeth with a pin from his table. Not a good sign. It is one of those lulls when nothing much happens. We are sitting around and waiting for crime to walk in; it usually does. Post-lunch, the police station has a warm dullness and the only sound comes from the ceiling fan grating its way around. At times like these you needed something to pick on, to sink your teeth into. Murthy seems headed for the dentist.

'No thakaraar happening?' he asks.

'No boss. Day off, for low life.'

'I have a theory,' says the boss. He examines a bit of his lunch that he has worried out of his molars. 'If you cannot find a motive for a crime, then it has to be an inside job.'

I keep my counsel. Murthy doesn't need it.

'I see you are lost as usual. In India there is no truly random senseless crime. We don't have those kind of idiots here.'

I had seen enough stupid people, the ones that got caught.

'You mean every crime is for gain or due to some loss?'

'Absolutely. Either material gain or emotional loss.'

'I still do not get it. Are you saying that if we do not have an angle or motive for a crime, then we should dig deeper among the insiders?'

'Yes. Most unsolved cases are because of letting insiders off the hook.'

'And what is your mantra, boss? I am sure you have one.'

'Yes, in fact, I do. It is simple. Do the unexpected and the improbable will reveal itself.'

And use some third degree, I mutter to myself. I have always noticed that we are very soft on those who are directly affected by a crime and come down hard on the outsiders, so to speak. We have a round of tea and biscuits.

* * *

My papa is a big man. When I stand near him I reach his knees. When he wears shoes and comes home he looks bigger. When he talks he smells. He shouts loudly. My mother never gets angry.

I like school. I like my brother. He likes windows. He writes in a notebook called diary.

My father balances me on his knee and teaches me Tamil. My mother's name is Kazhuthai.

* * *

I wonder what we would have done without television. During the day my mother watches a number of serials. The volume is always high as she often moves from room to room busying herself in her daily routine. But it doesn't matter as the whole building seems to follow the same serials. After a while I usually shut the door and stay in my room.

I want to talk to my mother; have a serious discussion. For some reason the difficult things in our family are never discussed. She still thinks I am a kid, a small fellow. I want to talk to her about Dad. She does not notice that it is getting worse. I can see it happen as I see things around me, I notice changes.

My Dad was always a big person. He had a large frame and big hands. He had a surprisingly gentle manner, till he got his hands on quarters of brandy. It used to be just weekends earlier. He would almost go through four quarters on Friday and Saturday evening. We knew when he was back as he would try and beat the door down. He would never use the bell. My sister, my little one, would be shaking. I would hold her hand.

The last two years have been really bad. The drinking is getting worse and it is on most days. For some reason he now uses the bell. When he gets into the house he has a lot of demands. My mother runs around, trying to keep pace. My sister stays in the other bedroom. I keep out of the way but hear every sound. It is mostly a loud monologue and many things being thrown around. I hold my watch in my hand and wait for my father to fall asleep.

One weekend my father was travelling. This was very rare. It was then that I got to talk to my mother. She was very hesitant at first but the nature of my questions surprised her. She thought I did not know what was going on. How could we not? She was beginning to fear for all of us for the first time. He never used to hit my mother earlier. But in the last two years he had started pushing her around and then the bruises started to show. And always when he was done he would go to the balcony and stand tall. He would smoke a cigarette and lean out and spit below.

* * *

My brother is kind. He holds my hand. I help him. He has strong hands. He has a cycle at home. It has four wheels. Mama says he has legs. I cannot see them. He does not walk. My father says my Mama is a pei-pishaash and my brother is a pichai.

* * *

It started as a case of accidental death. There was a hysterical call around eleven at night. A man had fallen off a balcony ledge three-storeys high. We had reached within ten minutes. The building watchman was an elderly fellow. He was shaking when we arrived. We went to the rear of the building and there in the open car park was the body of a big-built male who seemed to have fallen directly onto the concrete floor. We cleared the place of the building residents and spoke to a doctor from the building. Not much in it, it seemed. Death was from impact. There were some cigarette butts around. It was obvious from the smell around him that the dead man had been drinking. The autopsy confirmed later that the man was drunk.

When they turned the body face upwards we saw him. It was our friend and foe, Gangadharan.

It was a moment. Senior Inspector Murthy was a man divided and his face reflected mixed emotions. What he was searching for was a tinge of regret.

I was hoping he wouldn't speak but he did.

'This is manifest destiny,' he said.

That turned a screw in my head. I realized that sometimes a man must die to enable us to see the life he led.

We went up the lift to his house. It was a nice breezy apartment with large windows opening out into the streets below and a round balcony in the living room from where the man seemed to have fallen. The wife was dishevelled but coherent. She had dark circles under her eyes and what seemed like some bruised discolouration under one eye and on her hands. There was a crippled son in a wheelchair, a nice-looking young man who spoke very good English. There was also a younger daughter, a school-going child. We went through the standard routine of questions. Not much love lost here it seemed from the body language. We spent time at the apartment and then did the rounds with the neighbours and then the watchman.

The next day we had a briefing with Murthy. I was keen on getting this over with as it seemed like a simple accident case. His starting line was his usual surprising best.

'So who are the usual suspects?'

'Suspects? It seems a straightforward accident. A drunk leans too far and falls off.'

'We shall see. Gangadharan was known to drink almost all evenings. He was a large fellow with a heavy build. It is not easy for him to have merely toppled over. Let us for the moment pursue other possibilities. Do we have any possible motives?'

'There are some possibilities. He was not an ideal father and the family was bearing the brunt of his behaviour.'

'You mean domestic violence?'

'Yes, there was that. The neighbours say he was a regular bully and they could hear most of what was going on. He was coming down hard on his wife in the last few months.'

'So the wife could have done something?'

'Well, she had the motive but from what we have gathered, she was with the neighbours when this took place. She seemed to have stepped out to borrow something. That's what she said.'

'You checked this with the neighbours?'

'Yes. She was with them. But it seems she had actually run across to escape from the bully. The guy seemed to have been going at her that night.'

'Has she done this before?'

'No. This was a first.'

'Were there any visitors?'

'Yes, there were. Some people from a real estate agency had visited in the half hour before this happened. There was an argument between them and they claimed to have left before this happened. A neighbour and the watchman say they saw them leave but we do not have a tight fix on the timings. From what we have, they had every reason to see him live. They were getting some payments out.'

'So who was with him, when he tumbled over?'

'The son was with him. It seems that when the wife and daughter came into the room they found the son on the floor near the balcony bruised and shaking. He had fallen off his wheelchair.'

'And what does the young fellow have to say?'

'Well, we actually have two versions; one which he told his mother and one which he told us. He told us he had fallen asleep and must have fallen off as he dreamt. It seems he dreams of running.'

'And what did he tell his mother?'

'That is a strange one. He told her that he was very disturbed about his father hitting her. He knew his physical condition and his medical bills were a big issue. He said he had tried to go over the balcony himself and had fallen from his chair in the process. His father, it seems, had tried to save him and had fallen over.'

Murthy made a noise. 'And you still want to close this case as a simple accident?'

'Boss, the boy is under heavy medication and one of the side effects is hallucination. He comes up with some strange ones anyway.'

'Like what?'

'Like his father blocking his view at nights. Stuff like that.'

'What about the neighbours? Have you covered them?'

'We have drawn a blank there. No angles, no motives and seemingly no access.'

'All right, let us leave it there. What do you recommend?'

'I suggest we close.'

Murthy looked long and hard at the mirror and bared his lips. A neat row of sparkling teeth. He had been to the dentist. He grinned at me.

'Let us go to the building one last time.'

* * *

I had a dream last night. My brother walked. I saw him. I was hiding.

* * *

Four Quarters is quiet. I broke my watch the night my father died. I cannot recall how. I was asleep that night, I think. Must have dozed off waiting for my father to turn in. I missed the commotion when it happened. My little sister and my mother helped me onto my chair. Seemed I had fallen off. It has happened before. I guess I get so fed up sometimes that when I dream, I see myself running free in the open fields, like a horse. I probably start off from my chair and try to run and then I fall as I dream.

Two police people came by today. They were very gentle and quiet. They spoke softly to my mother. I like the one they call Murthy. He is older and very smart. He leant forward as he spoke and comforted my mother as she cried softly. My sister was peeping out from behind the curtains and the other officer played with her. She ran away into the bedroom.

They came towards me and wheeled me next to my mother. Mr Murthy shook my hand.

'You have a strong grip, son.'

'Thank you, sir.'

'Where did you get that bruise?'

'I fell off the chair.'

'Does that happen often?'

'No sir, only when I dream.'

'And what do you dream of, my son?'

'I dream of running, running wild.'

'I understand. But see where it got you, down on the floor and hurt bad.'

'Sure it did, sir. But at least I was better off than my father that night.'

'And how is that?'

'He dreamt he could fly.'

'What?'

'That night on the balcony he told me he had a dream that he could fly.'

'Fly? He must have been really drunk. What did you tell him?'

'I told him I believed him. And could you please show me. And before I knew it he was gone.'

* * *

We had a quiet ride back to the station. Murthy looked lost for words. Somewhere along the way he started to laugh and kept laughing till the tears flowed down his cheeks. I must confess I was grinning myself.

'What do we have here?' he asked.

'Not much, boss. I think we need to take that boy in and work him over.'

And here we had an unwritten disagreement. Senior Inspector Murthy felt that justice had been served. He was done with the case. I could see that.

'Do you know what you will get from the boy?' he asked. 'Three more stories, each better than the other.'

We reached the station and that evening I worried about what to do next. I couldn't sleep that night if I decided to close that file. Murthy came up to me.

'I have a bad feeling,' I told him.

He shrugged. He couldn't impose on me to close the file. He has never stopped trying to teach me the importance of the practical and the expedient.

'I got a call from the wife,' he said. 'She has donated a heap of small currency to the Police Fund.'

I could sense what he was hinting at.

'So you suggest I ...'

He nodded and smiled.

I shut the file ceremonially but did not put it away. It lay where I could retrieve it. Murthy Sir looked at the pile of pending files disdainfully. He feels I collect them. I feel he resolves things in his head.

That evening a new Tamil film released all over the state. It was a comedy but for some reason it wasn't funny. We were at the matinee show a row behind Gangadharan's family. The two children laughed at the funny bits and the mother cried through them. At one point the boy turned around and looked into my eyes. He held my gaze. I understood something that day. The film was called Uthama Puthiran; loosely translated that means 'The Best Son'.

VIII

THE CONFESSION

'WHERE ARE YOU FROM, KUMAR?'

My forefathers were Mittals, Guptas and Agarwals. They chose to break away from Uttar Pradesh and travel to remote places with their wits. They did better than survive. Each of them moved South and established a first generation business. My family tree resembles a weed that wanders at will with no pomp and very little visibility. It is hardy, unfussy, ignored, occasionally uprooted and the first to revive. Among birds we are like the crow. We forage rather than sing songs.

'What business?'

Adaptation.

'Funny.'

Our business is mostly food. Sweetmeats and savouries adorn our daily living; sohan-papdi, Mysore pak and laddoos made from pure ghee. Amidst them some khara-boondi and ompodi. We also made the best dosas in the land, better than the locals. After two generations our skin had darkened, our names bore the initials of our fathers like the Southerners, we knew the local language and we practised the local customs. We knew the deities in the Big Temple, Srirangam and Chidambaram. We paid more to the poosaris and got better darshans. Some of us could even pass off as Brahmins.

'So where are you from, Kumar?'

Can a question like this inhabit a page, breed stories and spell my raison d'être?

I could tell you the place of my birth, the land of my living and the logic of my existence. I have tried.

* * *

This is a familiar place, this police station in Kotturpuram. It abuts a bridge over the Adyar River which, despite its average height is a site for suicides. Young people fling themselves over in some throe or the other and find stones below that do the job. The nearby road is a place for lesser planned accidents. I have stood here often with no agenda. Some government housing rises near the banks and affronts anyone with clear eyes. I am not offended. It takes more. It takes a bus-load more to get my attention.

The police station is offensive. This is a protectorate of crass and its creed. The building is painted a bright red, made of bricks that are plastered over but for some reason they are outlined and highlighted with white paint and look like Phantom's undies. Two jeeps are parked outside the building. They have POLICE stencilled all over in red and a rotating red light atop the vehicles. The constabulary doesn't believe in subtlety in its precincts.

Words come cheap in this place. Ask me. People shout, scream and lather. Fragments of conversations can be heard from a handset in the front seat. Somewhere in the vicinity and in a slummy neighbourhood a quarrel has turned ugly.

This is the abhang that plays in my head.

'Kripa karo,' I mumble.

A constable hears me.

'Innada?' he queries. 'Speaking Hindi? Porikki,' he adds.

Bugger has bluster, his place has bustle. I cannot get my eyes off his pants; they are tight; there is no room to manoeuvre. Do not scratch, I urge him. He does. He is in a hurry.

'Wait here,' he tells me.

'Don't go anywhere,' he adds.

He speaks in instalments.

Everything is urgent in this cop-house. People come looking frantic and expect quick redressal. The accused lie in cells, looking listless. I am curious. I want to walk up to them and check the soles of their feet for torture. That's where they do it I have heard. It still hasn't sunk into my head that I too belong here in the garb of an accused, a man caught off-kilter, bearing motive.

I have been given pride of place at the centre of Inspector Murthy's cabin. They have made me stand. Two constables guard the door with their lathis. They look bored. I fall asleep.

'You have come here before,' says Murthy. 'I have seen the records.'

Inspector Murthy is in my face and it is not a pleasant sight. He is breathing heavily and his banian is wet. I can smell Margo soap, a neem cake prescribed for sensitive skins.

'Don't waste my time,' he says. We have barely begun.

'What are your particulars?' he asks.

Particulars? Now I remember the things that brought me here. A man called Balan had suffered at my behest. I had skinned the bugger and felt his hide. I had suffered too at the hands of the anonymous who spring up in streets for defending the fallen. They had lain about my face and my hands and legs. I had recuperated in this police station.

'Manslaughter,' says Murthy. He looks impressed. 'You killed a man over a motorbike accident. On the record you said it was a misunderstanding over language and that you knew Tamizh while your victim...'

'...knew only Tamil and thought I knew only Hindi. That is an old case,' I protest.

'What about your wife?'

What about her?

'Ms Sandhya was hale and hearty and one day she disappears into thin air? All we recovered was a car on Marina Beach and two empty beer bottles.'

Could she have drowned, Inspector?

'You took three days to file a Missing Person report. Why?'

She was a strong swimmer. She would not give up easily.

I remember her face, framed, her arms tanned, the perfume where she lay and the warmth of her embrace. I remember her silence, her imprudent pauses and her fondness for mandarin in all shapes and sizes.

'We were estranged,' I mumble. 'She was going away all the time.'

'Again no proper explanation; you stayed together in the same house. Neighbours said it was peaceful. There were no fights.'

It was a small matter, Inspector. Small thinking, small pleasures and a litany of small-sized woes.

'I find in you all that is unusual,' says Murthy. 'You are a riddle, like a person with many faces. Now you are here because another man has disappeared into thin air. Ramanathan.'

He looks at the form that has been filled, the register of record and he laughs.

'Writer?' he queries. 'You are a writer?'

'Merely spill-over,' I reply. 'All that I cannot hold in my head.'

'While you were here we went to your house and raided it. We found all your papers, these details.'

He reads carelessly, flipping pages.

'Everything you have narrated...'

'Is fiction,' I reply.

Before me are sheets of paper tied together by a rubber band and there is a bound ledger in which I have inscribed events. My shoulders are aching and I have a sore behind.

'Your friend Rangaswamy is here with his wife.'

Wife? Yes, of course, a fragrant flower called Kasturi. I have not met him in a while.

I need a drag. I need Rangaswamy and his stash. Murthy is reading my sheets and frowning.

'Why do you sign off as Valiban?'

* * *

There is no greater art than seduction. This was another homily from Ranga. He should know. He says I have done it with a pen, an implement he never needed. I am past feeling. In my mind is a staircase and a poem by Kennedy. I walk down and four men follow me home: Ramanathan, Valiban, Rangaswamy and Kumar.

That first night they got after my soles. I wept. I feel inconsolable when someone is beating my feet and nobody cares. The whole fucking thing plays out in my head. I lose track. It is like a dressage performance; men astride animals jumping over bones. There is no threshold to pain. Murthy, you bastard, you should know. Authorship is not a good bedrock for a confession. I confessed; over and over to many crimes.

'Where is your wife Sandhya?' asks Murthy for the nth time. 'How could she just go missing? You want me to believe that story?'

I shrug and it hurts.

'Can you hear me? Where is she, where have you hidden her?'

'She is buried in my garden in a house in Cenotaph Road next to her dog amidst the shrubbery she loved.'

He laughs.

'Should I go dig for her?'

I nod. He should. He should join the long list of diggers.

'You might find water,' I mumble. 'Or you might find a dog.'

'We could not find your wife's will. Did she leave one?'

'Who wants to know?' I ask.

'Her family, who else? Someone called Athimber and someone called Mapilai.'

Now everything makes sense. The fuckers are after the house I am staying in and this Murthy must be doing their bidding.

'Why do you sign these stories as Valiban? Who is Valiban? Are those stories real?'

'Of course not,' I reply.

He waves a piece of paper at me.

'How did you get this death certificate of Mr Ramanathan?'

I suppress a smile. A piece of paper can prove a man existed. A death certificate can create a life. What the fuck is fiction if I can make you believe? Should I tell him that this was a trial run and what I was preparing for was for my wife's certificate?

'Murthy sir. What do you want from me? I have nothing else.'

There was blood by now and he had seen it. He takes a break from his browbeating.

'Write your confession and sign it,' he says.

I write. My hands are shaking and my mind is a mess. This is the time to write. This is the truth. How do I say this?

I hand him the folded sheet ceremoniously. He leads me out of his inner courtyard into his chamber where I sit. I must look like a mess because he is staring at me.

'What?'

He smiles. 'You look like a chef who has parted with his recipe.'

The bastard is in for a surprise. I wasn't going to confess to anything. He opens the page and reads. There will be Hell to pay once he is done.

Toe upon toe, a snowing flesh,
A gold of lemon, root and rind,
She sifts in sunlight down the stairs
With nothing on. Nor on her mind.
We spy beneath the banister

A constant thresh of thigh on thigh.
Her lips imprint the swinging air
That parts to let her parts go by.
One-woman waterfall, she wears
Her slow descent like a long cape
And pausing, on the final stair
Collects her motions into shape.

* * *

I guess I died at that place. The physical commotion must have done me in. No one can endure this pummelling and survive. They left me in police custody for another 24 hours in which time Murthy's assistant, a constable called Perumal was asked to soften me up further. Perumal is lanky and loose-limbed and is forever flexing himself, cracking his knuckles, rotating his head and stretching his hamstrings. He keeps his muscles in shape and by the look of them he seems capable of squeezing life out of them as well. I would be putty. He leaps to his task.

The whole of last night Perumal was at my feet beating them. He was good at this job. He used a leather strap with knots at the end to whack my soles. Then he kneaded me in places where my nerve ends met. After a few minutes he grew tired of my bleating and he cupped his left palm, placed it over my mouth and continued with one hand. This brought tears to my eyes. It reaffirmed my faith in humanity that this ogre could not bear to hear me scream.

When he took a break to towel himself down I told him what I felt was his enduring quality. 'Naale ka keeda hai tu.'

He didn't comprehend my Hindi. He merely snorted, flexed his arms and readied himself.

'Bhosadi ki aulad hai tu,' I added softly.

I remember hallucinating and blurting out my innermost secret to him.

'I wish most to put a danda up your gaand.'

He still didn't get it.

'Dai, pushnika,' I called him finally.

He smarted at being called a pumpkin. He continued with renewed vigour.

'Thevadiya magan,' said Perumal when he was finally done.

'Madarchod,' I replied feebly. I felt I would never walk again.

The next morning my friend Ranga came and I asked him for help. He laughed. He said I wasn't helping my own case and was forever pushing a self-destruct button.

'Poetry as confession? I am proud of you, son. What the fuck were you thinking?'

He had spirited in some rum and a loose-packed cigarette. It served as Communion.

'You look like a paavum,' he said. 'You want a mirror?'

No. I could see what they had done to my hands and legs.

'I believe last night you lectured the cops on their need to study Hindi? Read it and write it, you said. Write your names down in it you said. And you called them illiterates. Unpadh is the word you used?'

I inhaled and the grass took hold and I felt distanced from the surroundings.

'Ranga, I have reached a stage where watching a bird build a nest moves me. Looking at an ant carrying a titbit into an anthill is suddenly life-affirming.'

Ranga smiled. We sat and puffed for a while, holding smoke as long as we could and breathing lines.

'This is good shit. I think I should go now. I am glad they are putting you away for a while. You have hung around us long enough.'

'Like a retired metaphor?'

'Like a fucking allegory.'

Grass makes us all poets.

'Mapilai and Athimber want your blood,' said Ranga. 'Looks like they are getting it.'

They want the fucking house, Rangaswamy, you know it. And you are torn between them and me because you are a good man.

Murthy came in and shook hands with Ranga trying not to greet him in too friendly a manner. They spoke softly.

'He is like my thambi,' said Ranga. It sounded like a plea on my behalf.

Murthy shrugged and shook his head. 'I asked him for his papers. And he gave me these stories,' he complained. 'Are these his bona fides?'

Ranga laughed and Murthy joined in.

'He is a writer,' said Ranga looking at me. They laughed some more.

Thankfully they left after arguing for a while and I wrote just to stay sane.

Thoughts sidle up to me like photographs. I have a handsome memory for faces, for people, especially their vices and their quirks. I believe in close-ups. Dusk is the time when her face returns. Sandhya comes and visits me in the evening. She is troubling. She has and always had just one question:

'Tonight, amidst my lapels and my folds, will you be bold?'

She mocks me. I, the thinker, the one she left because I was never good enough. I am in a state she never truly was: properly fucked.

* * *

I dreamt of death that night.

Dai Ranga, wotha koodi. Or as Ramanathan would put it mildly: badwa rascal. You are the son of a friendly whore who wore specs one day, looked up at a man and saw a fucking husband. Take that. I wish I was a traveller like you, who breathes air from wind. Come now, dig up that conch shell and blow my shankha. They are dancing in the streets, strewing rose petals and bursting crackers. The pot of water is ready. They have come to take me away. I hate leaving.

The bedecked pushcart is at my door, waiting, aware of my infirmity. It has a shaky poster bed of flowers. Wrapped in white I am hoisted up on the shoulders of strangers. I am bathed clean, anointed, with cotton in my nostrils and hair neatly combed over a cold skin. The rudaalis wail, a few well-paid ones beat their breasts. And the traffic parts as we swing along down Radhakrishna Salai. Two street kids dance, their shorts held by string, their skin strung over bones. One bare-chested man beats a drum. The song is gaana, the dance is koothu and I am a baniya in the wrong place and time in the guise of a Tamizha. This is a crazy, fucking country. At the ghat they light me up. Ranga smokes and watches and pours some oil.

Tomorrow the Nagarpalika that polices rubbish will fell all the langda trees that drink up precious water and bear no mangoes. And a street dog that went to the pound will dream of Nizamuddin and the days when haleem was served by the gram. The music will be the blues. I hope to be remembered in this street amongst the lame as the husband of the one with amorous thoughts and sexy legs. 'There used to be a writer here in this empty house,' they will say. 'He had a porous mind.'

MY DEAR MURTHY

MURTHI: A handmade stone in the likeness of someone you don't know.

* * *

Dear Murthy,

This is what I have always wanted to do: walk into a temple like Tirupati, stand in line for hours with a token, feel one with people I do not know, jostle, stand on my toes and peer, get into the sanctum barefoot and bare head, holding something of value, in my case a paper and pen; and then when I get my private audience with you for a fleeting moment I want to do no more than address a letter as such.

* * *

Thiru Murthy,

You who made this Earth, are now before me; Thiru Murthi of 3rd Cross, Fourth Main; they have made a small house for you, which I enter from a side lane past a middle-aged bhakt who is gathering vegetables for an avial. The flower-seller is mean looking and the poosari inside your house is unkempt. This is a Civil Service neighbourhood where buildings are called Kailash and Mansarovar but the plate is dented and the pickings are meagre. Thiru Murthi, are you well, amongst these stray dogs and crows that have made this their home?

* * *

Dear Sambasiva Murthy,

I came late and you were locked in. The iron slide gate was locked but I could see your sanctum door that bore a Godrej padlock. Nobody will steal you away today, not even the slacker sleeping outside your door. If I ever saw you eye to eye, you would walk away with me. I swear. But you never look me in the eye. Why? I know the sculptor who made you, a young huckster, a coward who thought infinity was the separation between two eyes.

So how do I address you? It can only be like this.

* * *

Dear Narayana Murthy,

A cretin asked me a question today. He said why did you write these stories? Why did you try to pre-empt your life? Look, what has happened is what you wrought.

This question came from a policeman. I told him why do you sing to the Lord? One day he will listen, and then? Why do you try to pre-empt your death?

* * *

Dear Inspector Murthy,

You asked me to write something for you, perhaps you asked in jest in the company of that jester, Ranga. I took it seriously. Ranga and I once went to Sri Lanka. It was a trip with a singular purpose. There is a piece of land in the midst of this country where many kingdoms marked their history. It is a small tract and yet it attracted us. One of these kingdoms had a monarch who set out to build his quarters atop a rock. This rock was hard to get to for anybody. The place is called Sigiriya. We wanted to climb that rock and visit this monarch. We wanted to see his living quarter up-close.

We did so. And once we climbed this windswept place we found no sharp edges. The wind had rounded off everything. The place was a ruin but it had enough to remind us that this chap Kasyapa lived well and lived perhaps by himself. He was here it seemed not to protect himself from marauders but to be by himself. And this was curiously attractive. This proposition was what pulled me here. For me this is the essential nature of man, to be by himself. Ours is the nature of singularity. There is no social animal I know of. There is pretence. As you grow old it is not very desperate to announce that in my world there is only me.

Murthy sir, this house on Cenotaph Road is my kingdom. That is what I wanted to say. It is my living quarter. Nobody can take it away from me. Not you with your native intelligence, nor your flunky Perumal with his thong. Ranga once told me that I was a stray and there is no place where I will belong. I will take my chances. A man like me has to.

* * *

At 5 a.m. the burly Murthy arrives with two of his young constables. I half expected a hangman with a rope. Murthy opens the cell door and keeps it open, pointedly. The way out of the station is clear. It is still dark outside and the street is quiet and empty. They stand me up, I pinch myself and in their sullen presence I realize I am still alive. I smell of sweat. The morning is my productive moment, a time when ideas occur and words spill out.

'Does the butcher find expression with a knife?' I ask the constable next to me.

It is my friend Perumal the dhur. I notice he has a pencil moustache, a junior accessory unlike Murthy, his boss, who has a luxuriant handlebar. He is searching my pockets and patting me down.

'Do you use a thong to express yourself?' I ask him. He wants to do so now. I can feel it.

He stays impassive, the young fellow. His colleague returns my belongings which had been confiscated. He makes a small mountain of my wallet, some change, a small pen and my notepad. I keep talking.

'I am reminded of water that collects every now and then near a drain; it swirls, eddies and just when it has shown you a form it disappears. My possessions are like that sometimes.'

I wish Perumal would acknowledge my presence. I am not a lifeless form, I wish to tell him. And you are not a Murti.

'What is the time?' asks Murthy.

'Five o' clock, sir,' says Perumal, looking at me with fixed eyes while he stuffs my belongings into my pockets. He stands back when he is done.

'Run,' says Murthy.

What?

'You heard me, run. Get out. Get away if you can.'

What will you do? I mean could you give me a hint?

'You have a headstart of a few minutes. Don't stop till you reach North India. There you will be safe.'

The two constables are young and fit and wide awake.

I stumbled but I ran. I ran out, paused, took a deep breath and a left turn, sprinted past the Kotturpuram Bridge, down the broad Sardar Patel Road and in the company of stray dogs I ran past the Saidapet Bridge. It was exhilarating. My lungs were hurting, my knees were hurting and my bare feet were past feeling by now. At some point I would falter but who cared. I was still alive. If the cops caught up with me, I would climb a tree. In the meanwhile I was going nowhere. This was my fucking place, this beach where you could sink or swim, where you could drink the air, bury your feet and cheat the tide.

Later, much later the voices came. Two people who should never have met spoke up as if to appease the pain.

'Life is so well behaved,' said Sandhya, half in wonder and half in regret.

'It's these damn memories that are wild,' said Ranga.

* * *

PARIKRAMA

I had my old man by the sea. He was a traditional thatha, not a grumpus, just an old fellow who showed his age by walking bent, not fighting frail nor pretending that his hands did not shake on their own. He would stand facing the eastern horizon every morning, genuflecting a little awkwardly, knocking his temples with his fists and awakening a few gods like Muruga and Paramasivan. I would be playing cricket on the sandy beach with the colony boys and preparing for my daily fight with the neighbourhood bully, a doughty kuppam dweller with muscle and height and the charisma of a gladiator. Bully and I would fight for territory, the only place on that beach that had firm sand where the ball would bounce. I would always lose. I would end up below him with sand in my hair and his muck in my face. His friends would cheer. Mine had no fight in them. My friends were college lads from a Jesuit Institution, accustomed to whatever was heaped on them. Thatha had his agenda and he would watch feebly as I suffered another of my moments.

Sleep falling. Dazed, confused and yet committed to this, day after day. Something brings me to trouble spots, places that do me harm. I like the silence that precedes mayhem.

Bully gets off my chest and I breathe again. He dusts himself down and spits by my side and he looks at Thatha with the slightest hint of apology. He plonks his stumps on the firm patch like he is claiming territory on the moon while we slink away to a sandy strip where the batsmen were at the mercy of bowlers who bowled shooters, powder-puff deliveries called uruttals that landed and skidded, kissed your ankles and broke your stumps.

I want to do more, resolve this issue once and for all. Moments like these and I have no inkling of what I will do to people who come in the way.

A pure moment is when it is about to happen and you know the before and you can imagine the hereafter. I imagine the second before my plane fell out of the sky. I was strapped in it. I think of the bomb that went off next to me. Would I know it did? What terrifies me is the thought that nothing happens. Life feels less lived somehow.

One day I shout at Thatha as I lie defeated. He walks up and lends a hand. I refuse it. This lifetime eater of parboiled rice snickers, showing gaps in his teeth. He offers his hand again and this time I see how frail he is. I grip it and haul myself up. He stays standing, somehow.

'Why do you keep coming back?' he asks. It is a fair question. 'You know why he comes, don't you?'

I shrug some sand off my shirt. I need breakfast, not philosophy.

'Why don't you counterpunch? I thought North Indians had fight.'

Hand to hand I would lose every time. There had to be another way.

Thatha is an advice monger, a sweet old man who preys on the young. Among the pattani sundal vendors he has packaged advice to offer.

'It is easy for you to say,' I tell him, as we walk towards the road marking our footsteps in the sand.

'Kanna,' he calls me, placing a hand on my shoulder. 'Fear comes from memory. Erase it like the sea does, a day at a time.'

'And belief? Where do I get that?'

He has the answers. 'It comes from lack of knowledge.'

'Is that why we go the temple?'

He laughs. 'You don't look like a temple-goer.'

We walk past a broken beer bottle and some paper plates still stained from last night's revelry.

'Forget God,' he says. 'He is a trouble-maker. He is my bully.'

We reach the car park. I dust my feet and prise out the sand between my toes. Thatha watches me. He has something more to say. I know what he is after. Thatha thinks he owns this patch of beach that adjoins his colony. And these kuppam boys shit on it every morning when the tide comes in and sometimes when the tide goes out. It is not a pleasant sight I am sure, watching this every day; people crouching in your sea-view and making small gopurams in the sand. Thatha is toilet-trained. He is also a sanctimonious Brahmin with a visceral lineage. I see him skating on the thin ice of middle class, watching a granddaughter suffer at the hands of a Reservation Policy that denied her a college seat to the likes of these very kuppam dwellers. But why pick on Bully? I guess it is because he makes a large gopuram. And then without washing his hands he walks up to Thatha's gate and makes eyes at his granddaughter every other day.

'Kanna.'

'Yes.'

'The day you realize you are no less, he will be no more.'

And Thatha's eyes twinkle. He is evil genius.

‘Could that day be arranged?’ I ask him.

‘Yes,’ he tells me as I start my car. ‘Yes,’ he adds for emphasis. He peers into my window. ‘His name is Balan. He rides a bike and you drive a car.’

I understood what he meant and, curiously, I knew what I had to do. It was as if my past was coming up to meet me. It was time for my perimeter run, my parikrama. Balan would pay and so would I. As I drove to Rainbow Colony I realized how much of my own life I held in my hands. I have to say Sandhya said it better the day she went missing. She wrapped an air of mutiny around her and said nothing.

According to ragpickers’ lore I am the last of a curious breed, one that bears resemblance to the street where I live. They call me the scion of this small lane where trees are held up by wires and pavements have been walked on by roads. The street where I live has blood. All the battles take place here. It is laughable. The territory is meek and the spoils are rotten but the dogs are hungry for love. So a chase and a skirmish helps, even if the prize is a mongrel. It gives meaning to life on that street. And it courses your blood.

I ran over a leg today. I was driving a small car that has a large A pillar. The funny thing is I didn’t feel a thing.

ACKNOWLEDGEMENTS

1. The quote by Jeanette Winterson in the book is an extract from 'Psychometry of Books from Art Objects' reprinted by permission of Peters Fraser and Dunlop (www.petersfraserdunlop.com) on behalf of Jeanette Winterson.
2. The two lines from the poem 'An Eastern Ballad' are by Allen Ginsberg published inter alia in *Collected Poems (1947-97)* by Harper Perennial as part of their Modern Classic series.
3. The poem 'Nude descending a Staircase' is by X.J. Kennedy and is from the book, *Nude Descending a Staircase: Poems, Songs, a Ballad* by X.J. Kennedy; published by Carnegie Mellon University Press.
4. Portions of this book were written at Sangam House, a writing residency near Nrityagram, Bangalore. Thanks are owed to Arshia Sattar and Lynn Fernandes and everyone else at Kula and Nrityagram.
5. The descriptions of nightfall and the treatment and medications mentioned are extracted from www.hashim.com. (Partly cached)

6. Thanks to Vivek Vilasini for permission to use a variation of his work 'Creation of Adam after Michelangelo': Archival print on Hanemuhle Photo Rag, 52*104 inches, 2009.